I0779949

PULP Literature

PULP Literature

PULP LITERATURE PRESS

Issue No. 46, Spring 2025

Publisher: Pulp Literature Press; Editor-in-Chief: Jennifer Landels; Acquisitions Editor: Mel Anastasiou; Senior Editor: Sierra Louie; Poetry Editors: Daniel Cowper & Emily Osborne; Copy Editor: Amanda Bidnall; Proofreader: Sierra Louie; Graphic Design: Amanda Bidnall & Sierra Louie; Cover Design: Kate Landels; Subscriptions: Carol McCauley; Advertising: Jared Schellenberg; First Readers: Amber Allen, Mark Cameron, Michaela Chan, Summer Keown, Sylvia Leong, Tara King. For advertising rates, direct inquiries to info@pulpliterature.com.

Cover painting, *Towton* by Steve R Gagnon. Illustrations for 'The Drift' by Jordan Bray. All other illustrations by Mel Anastasiou.

Pulp Literature: ISSN 2292-2164 (Print), ISSN 2292-2172 (Digital), Issue No. 46, Spring 2025.

Published quarterly by Pulp Literature Press, 21955 16 Ave, Langley, BC, Canada V2Z 1K5, pulpliterature.com, at $18.00 per copy. Annual subscription $60.00 in Canada, $80.00 in continental USA, $92.00 elsewhere. Printed in Surrey, BC, Canada, by Fraser Printers Ltd. Copyright © 2025 Pulp Literature Press. All stories and works of art copyright © 2025 their authors as per bylines.

Pulp Literature Press is based in the unceded traditional Coast Salish Territories of the Katzie, Kwantlen, Matsqui, and Semiahmoo First Nations.

Pulp Literature Press gratefully acknowledges the support of the Canada Council for the Arts and the Government of Canada.

Pulp Literature is a proud member of the Magazine Association of BC and Magazines Canada.

TABLE OF CONTENTS

FROM THE PULP LIT PULPIT

Transformation

This is a changeable season, isn't it? Bare branches bud, blossoms unfold, leaves extend, and the rain falls all around. Until … sunshine. There's always something going on. No wonder people talk about the weather. It never loses its intrigue. Spring tells a story of tiny and vast transformations. And, in the spirit of the season, our spring issue is full of great storytelling.

We're West Coast in origin and personality, and we love our contributors from across the nation. We publish largely Canadian stories and artwork, but alongside these, we also publish authors and artists from around the globe—not just because we love their work, but also because our Canadian stories thereby reach an epic readership in many countries.

Here are some now. We loved reading them, and we hope you do too.

~ *Mel Anastasiou*

In THIS ISSUE

Cover artist **Steve R Gagnon**'s raven calls across the Towton battlefield, summoning heroes in many guises.

In our feature story, 'The Storm Tastes of Freedom' by **Finnian Burnett**, and in 'Chardi Kala for the Modern Dirtbag' by **Kiran K Basra**, unlikely heroines fight through different realities for the lives they deserve.

Deception, skulduggery, and shifting personae abound in 'The Suicide Mission' by **KR Segriff**, and in 'Fire at the Castello' by **Mel Anastasiou**, the first instalment of a brand-new Monument Studios Mystery starring our favourite silver-screen sleuth, Frankie Ray.

Horror writers **EC Dorgan** and **Patrick Barb**, back for encore performances, continue to make us question identities and reality in 'The Myth of the Familiar' and 'Playdate', while family myths and truths loom large in 'The Orangery' by **Mark Gallacher** and Part 2 of 'Their Grandfather's Chair' by **JM Landels**.

This issue is also jam-packed with contest-winning heroes, from **Michael Carson**, whose 'Darth Vader vs Testicular

Cancer' kept the Jack Whyte Storyteller Award judges Diana Gabaldon and Donald Maass in stitches, to the sparkling Kingfisher poets **Sandra Kasturi, Angelle McDougall, Nicole Moen,** and **Callista Markotich,** to the Raven Contest high-flyers **Shanley Kearney** and **Emily Groot.**

And finally, we bring you a small, silent hero who makes his way through a strange and beautiful world in Part 2 of *The Drift*, written and drawn by **Jordan Bray.**

Gird your loins, brave readers, and step into universes of wonder!

THE STORM TASTES OF FREEDOM

Finnian Burnett

Finnian Burnett *is an author whose writing explores intersections of mental health, gender identity, disability, and life in a fat body. Their work has appeared on CBC Books, in Blank Spaces Magazine, Pulp Literature, and more. Finnian's most recent flash fiction collection, The Price of Cookies, is available from your local library and wherever books are sold, and you can find their stories in Pulp Literature issues 37, 41, and 43. When not writing or teaching, Finnian watches too much Star Trek and futilely tries to grow a garden.*

©2025, Finnian Burnett

The Storm Tastes of Freedom

Act 5. **The search encompasses** the east woods, the back of the old motel where high-school kids' frantic whispers scratch across each other's bodies on mouldy bedspreads, the airport. They search behind the bushes where they'll find condom wrappers, needles, and the pink blazer Kevin Clarence buried after killing his wife. Maybe the bike path along Muller's fields. The search ends there, but, after a tip, a squad car goes to your father's home where officers arrest him, though they never find your body.

Act 4. A hole in time and space, and you don't know if she's real or not, but the chance to escape is this doorway, this light—the glow shimmers on the wet rivulets cascading down your face, melting into pools in your valleys. *Taste freedom,* she says, and you stand in the threshold, rainy tendrils tickling your back, his voice behind you, hers ahead. You hover between here and there, between rough skin and soft lips, between remembering and projecting, and you step through without looking back.

Act 3. His car stops beside you—*get out of the storm, stupid girl.* There's no running, no escape. Move to his car, fingers outstretched to the handle, and his wolf smile glows in the electricity in the lightning. But there's something else, an opening, a portal, a chance. And she's there, woman to woman—*come with me*—her fingers touch your mouth with a warmth tasting of flight, currents, safety.

Act 2. Your lips open to the sky, drinking rain as it pours across your face and drenches your hair. The rain smells like freedom, like your future. The blurred shine of oncoming headlights dances across you as you spin and spin in the downpour until you finally stop, spent and soaking. You don't wonder if the headlights are his because you're a million miles away, safely in another world.

Act 1. He tells you he's coming for you once he watches the weather because there's a hell of a storm coming in and if he has to bring in the car, he wants to know right now. You know his mouth will taste of whiskey and bad luck, and you run to your room, but this time, you don't wait. You scurry through the window, climb down the drainpipe. You run through Muller's fields and your legs carry you all the way to the main road out of town, and by the time the storm breaks, you have become a force.

FEATURE INTERVIEW

Finnian Burnett

Pulp Literature: *As sombre as 'The Storm Tastes of Freedom' is, in a way it's about possibilities. We enter the narrative at its end, the possibility of escape presented to us almost from the start. Why was it important for you to structure this piece in this way?*

Finnian Burnett: I love experimenting with form, style, and language in flash. In this story, I really wanted to upend the idea of story structure while still leaving it ambiguous enough in the first paragraph to let the reader gradually come to the understanding that we're moving backward in time. I also wanted to lead with the main idea, which is that escape is possible. I think the structure of this story gives hope and, also, a sense of inevitability, which can make readers feel a little unsettled, which is my favourite way to make them feel.

PL: *On the topic of possibilities, what do you hope to make possible through your storytelling?*

FB: Authors always say to just write for yourself. And when I'm in draft mode, I do absolutely write for myself. I tend to not think of anything but the story. How can I get it across? Does it create an impact? What do the characters want to do? But after I write, when I'm sending it into the world, I do want it to land with my readers.

Whether they love it or not, if it challenges their assumptions about something, if it makes them think or feel, I feel I've been successful. Of course I want to be universally loved, unilaterally idolized, and irrevocably etched into the annals of history as a paragon of brilliance and charm. Who doesn't!? But I'll settle for writing stories that make me happy first, and then finding an audience who loves them almost as much as I do.

PL: *Despite its short length, this story makes space for exceptionally detailed and embodied imagery. It's overflowing with it. How do you determine which elements or techniques to prioritize when writing for short forms?*

FB: I don't know that I am that intentional about certain techniques most of the time. All of my flash stories are intuitive. While I may struggle over every word of a novel, flash fiction stories tend to pop out almost fully formed. When I'm editing, I look for strong verbs that convey movement and deeper details, colours, smells, sounds. Flash fiction is less about the traditional structure of a story and more about the feelings they evoke, so writing them from a place of intuition feels right to me. That said, I do revise stories. I look for character motivation, strong imagery, evocative language. I'll read it aloud to see if the flow feels right to me. Then I let it go and hope it lands with someone. I knew I was going to send this one to *Pulp Literature* before I even considered anywhere else because *Pulp Literature* isn't afraid to upend traditional story rules, which is something I love about you!

PL: *Following the publication of your second flash fiction novella,* The Price of Cookies, *what insight have you gained through the process of writing this collection and releasing it into the world? Any* *wisdom to share with fellow and aspiring authors?*

FB: More than anything else, I've learned that flash fiction is a valid path to success in the writing world. As someone with ADHD, depression, and a to-do list that verges on overwhelming most days, my ability to write long form is severely compromised much of the time. Flash fiction stories were a way for me to put the fun back into writing, to allow myself explorations with style, to play with words, to just remember how it feels to love writing. Turning flash pieces into a novella-in-flash gave me a book-length project which has led to so much success at writing conferences and teaching conferences, and as a keynote speaker for several organizations. I think I was always good at those things—just having a book made it easier to get the attention of many of the organizers.

For writers interested in flash fiction, my advice is to write, write, write. Play with words and have fun with it. And when you've found your voice, start submitting. Marion Lougheed, the head of Off Topic Publishing, reached out to me about publishing *The Price of Cookies* because she'd read other flash pieces I'd published. It's a great way to get your name and your words out there to the eyes of readers, publishers, conference organizers.

PL: *It's now been over a year since we were lucky enough to speak with you as our feature author for Issue 41. Could you tell us what you have been working on since then?*

FB: So much! I can't believe what a year it's been. I finished my full-length novel *Arthur Undressed*, based on a character created in my first novella-in-flash. I got an agent for that novel—my first-choice agent, the amazing and brilliant Stacey Kondla of The Rights Factory. I've completed two novels with my co-writer and bestie, Andrew Buckley. These queer, comedic Shakespeare retellings are with our agent, Terrie Wolf. And I've started a new book which is very slow going because I really believe I need to go live in a village in Scotland for three months as research for that one. I'm also very slowly working on a third novella-in-flash tentatively called *Red Shirts Sometimes Survive*. Two of the stories in this collection have appeared in *Pulp Literature* and one was shortlisted for the London Independent Story Prize. Another was published on the *Free Flash Fiction* site and Jonathan Frakes actually liked it on social media. All the flash fiction pieces are in some way tied to *Star Trek*. It's just been slow going because I am writing all microfictions for this one, so each story has to be under five hundred. And I want them to be perfect little punches of emotion like 'When Captain Picard Was My Dad', and I set the bar high with that one. So that may be published in 2 0 3 4 or something.

I'm also working on a non-fiction book with Andrew and I've just finished outlining a dystopian book about the last queer in the world. My scattered brain loves to chase the shiny, but I'm also aware that I must settle into a project in order to finish it.

PL: *Thank you so much for your time, Finnian, and we can't wait to see all these new projects on the shelves.*

SELECT BIBLIOGRAPHY

NOVELS

The Price of Cookies, Off Topic Publishing, 2 0 2 4
The Clothes Make the Man, Ad Hoc Fiction, 2 0 2 3
Coyote Ate the Stars (as EA Van Stralen), 2 0 1 8

SHORT STORIES AND POETRY

'Just a Touch', Five Minute Lit fall contest shortlist, 2 0 2 5
'How to Erase Indelible Ink from the Skin of Your Arms', Off
    Topic Publishing first-place winner, 2 0 2 4
'Adam's Side of the Gate', *Blank Spaces Magazine* first-place winner,
    2 0 2 4
'A Boy Like Bobby', Off Topic Publishing, 2 0 2 4
'Grandma Had Guns', *Pulp Literature* Issue 4 3, Summer 2 0 2 4
'When Captain Picard Was My Dad', *Pulp Literature* Issue 4 1,
    Winter 2 0 2 4
'Nothing Left' and 'Ethan's Pecs', *Pulp Literature* Issue 3 7, Winter
    2 0 2 3

THE 2024 KINGFISHER POETRY PRIZE

© 2 0 2 5, Sandra Kasturi, Angelle McDougall, Nicole Moen, Callista Markotich

THE 2024 KINGFISHER POETRY PRIZE

In 2 0 2 3, to celebrate ten years of *Pulp Literature*, we introduced the Kingfisher Poetry Prize. This year, we were thrilled to uncover yet another bounty of brilliant submissions. Thanks to our excellent first judges Emily Osborne and Daniel Cowper, and our final judge, the exceptional Jude Neale, we can now present the winners to you. Please find the four dazzling short poems that caught Jude's eye below.

Winner: 'Apiography: A Fragment' by Sandra Kasturi

'Apiography: A Fragment' transforms bees into calligraphers of existence. The title combines "apian" and "biography," hinting at a fleeting life inscribed mid-flight. Equally profound is "the hum of creation, the calligraphy of sleep," blending sound and vision to evoke Taoist dreams and the sacred rhythm of existence. This poem fuses beauty and philosophy in a luminous, ephemeral meditation.

First Runner-Up: 'Hideaway' by Angelle McDougall

'Hideaway' evokes a fleeting sanctuary from life's storms, where urgency and intimacy collide. The opening line, "While there's still time to run through the wheat fields ——", captures the poem's golden-hour vitality. Meanwhile, "angry clouds chase from the lightning-bright skies" mirrors nature's chaos and human emotion, blending beauty and tension seamlessly.

Second Runner-Up: **'What Else Am I Wrong About?' by Nicole Moen**

This poem turns a leaf into a mirror, reflecting the quiet assumptions that shape our gaze. "Why do I see this as upright?" it asks, unravelling the interplay of nature, orientation, and cultural symbol — a graceful meditation on perception.

Honourable Mention: **'My Dad John (Jack to Mom) Gives Medical History' by Callista Markotich**

This understated poem distills memory and loss into a poignant refrain. The line "Lou in bed, silent, shrunken, their mother weeping quietly at dawn" juxtaposes familial tenderness with the inevitability of mortality, encapsulating its emotional weight in just a few vivid strokes.

Congratulations are also in order for those who made the 2024 Kingfisher shortlist:

Diane Massam for 'Ground Cover'
Greer Shothers for 'The Integument Instructional'
Jordan Mounteer for 'Yew (Taxus brevifolia)'
Rhonda Collis for 'Dark Morning'
Sadie McCarney for 'Summer, Maybe'
Tara Seguin for 'Accord'

Sandra Kasturi *is a mixed-race poet, fiction writer, book reviewer, and former publisher. She has had two books of poetry published, both from Tightrope Books:* The Animal Bridegroom *and* Come Late to the Love of Birds. *Her work has appeared in:* Rattle, Contemporary Verse 2, The New Quarterly, ARC Poetry Magazine, Taddle Creek, Canadian Notes & Queries, Other Tongues: Mixed Race Women Speak Out, *various* Tesseracts *anthologies,* Postscripts to Darkness 6, Abyss & Apex, Amazing Stories, Evolve, Chilling Tales, Black Feathers, The Sum of Us, Shadows & Tall Trees, 8 0! Memories and Reflections on Ursula K LeGuin, Tales of the Unanticipated, Nuit Blanche, Annex Echo, On Spec, Gods, Memes and Monsters, *and more. Sandra has won the Whittaker Prize, ARC Magazine's Poem of the Year Contest, the Sunburst Award, and most recently, the Kingfisher Poetry Prize. She was a finalist for the National Poetry Series in 2024. Sandra is fond of red lipstick, gin and tonic, and Idris Elba.*

Angelle McDougall *is neurodivergent and a dedicated world traveller, a retired college instructor, a mother of adult sons, a graduate of the Writers Studio at SFU, and a loom-knitter. She lives in Edmonton and enjoys chronicling the fantastic adventures she shares with her author husband.*

Nicole Moen *(she/her) is the winner of* Island Writer Magazine's *2022 poetry contest. She was longlisted for the 2023 Magpie Award for Poetry and recently selected for Wordstorm's* Counterflow *magazine. Her poetry has been published in* The Purposeful Mayonnaise, *the anthology* Worth More Standing *from Caitlin Press, and the chapbook* Gathering Roots: Six Ancestral Land Acknowledgement Poems *through her own Woven Roots Press. Her creative non-fiction has appeared in* Focus on Women *and* Island Parent. *She lives on Lekwungen Homelands (Victoria, BC).*

*Poems by **Callista Markotich**, retired superintendent of education in eastern Ontario, appear in Canadian literary reviews from Arc to Vallum and from Vancouver BC, to Saint John's NL, and in a few American and British quarterlies and zines. Her poetry has received first- and second-place awards and honourable mentions, has been shortlisted, and has been recognized with Pushcart and National Magazine nominations. She is a contributing editor for Arc Poetry Magazine. Callista's debut collection, Wrap in a Big White Towel, was published by Frontenac House, 2024. She lives gratefully on the homeland of the Anishinaabe, Haudenosaunee, and Huron-Wendat in Kingston, Ontario, Canada.*

Apiography: A Fragment

by Sandra Kasturi

Bees write in the air as if it were parchment;
each flight a curve toward coneflower & goldenrod,
the upward stroke of a velvet ball gown.

Each black stripe on yellow-flocked abdomens,
a dip of a brush and swirl of Chinese characters —
the boy who drew bees, not cats.

In a parallel world, Zhuangzi dreams of bees
or the bees dream of him: the hum of creation,
the calligraphy of sleep.

Hideaway

BY ANGELLE MCDOUGALL

While there's still time to run
through the wheat fields —

tall stalks slapping our shins
and tugging at your dress.

While wind whooshes across our cheeks
and nectar-drunk bees

bumble after us, and angry clouds
chase from the lightning-bright skies —

take my hand and gallop with me
to the granary, to weather

the tempestuous storm together.

What Else Am I Wrong About?

BY NICOLE MOEN

I
snap
photos of
a single
leaf. Always
stem down, leaf
tip skyward.
Why do I
see *this* as upright?
Is stem a stand-in leg?
Is it the maple leaf orientation
on the flag of the collection
of peoples, and their
federated lands?
I'm content trusting
neither leaf
nor
tree
fret.

MY DAD JOHN (JACK TO MOM) GIVES MEDICAL HISTORY

BY CALLISTA MARKOTICH

The young oncologist asks: cancer in your family, John?
No, Dad says, and Mom, her hand on his, says gently: Jack.
Ah. Half-forgot: his sister Lou cartwheeling, laughing, on
    their lawn.
The young oncologist asks: cancer in your family, John?
Lou in bed, silent, shrunken, their mother weeping quietly
    at dawn,
a cheerless morning, a pallid sky, trees filigreed in black.
The young oncologist asks: cancer in your family, John?
No, Dad says, and Mom, her hand on his, says gently: Jack.

THE EXTRA TAKES THE CASTLE: A MONUMENT STUDIOS MYSTERY

Mel Anastasiou

Mel Anastasiou *writes the Fairmount Manor Mysteries, the Monument Studios Mysteries, and the Hertfordshire Pub Mysteries, available at pulpliterature.com. She won a Literary Titan Gold Book Award and was longlisted for the Leacock Memorial Medal for Humour for her novel* Stella Ryman and the Fairmount Manor Mysteries. *Look for* The Labours of Mrs Stella Ryman, *available through online booksellers and at Pulp Literature Press.*

The Extra Takes the Castle, *the second book in the Monument Studios Mysteries series, finds Frankie Ray and Connie Mooney settled soon after their previous entanglements with murder in Hollywood. Frankie is broke, and banned from Monument Studios, but there are adventures, obstacles, and deadly perils ahead for these two Vancouver hopefuls and all the extras at Paradise Gardens on Sunset Boulevard.*

©2025, Mel Anastasiou

The Extra Takes the Castle, Part 1: Fire at the Castello

The Castello Hotel stood six storeys tall on Sunset Boulevard. It catered to the great stars and greater has-beens and was staffed with Hollywood hopefuls. Frankie Ray intended to become part of it: today as a staffer and, in the fullness of time, as a star.

Frankie tipped back her head to take in the faux battlements ringing the Castello's top floor. The movement dislodged her borrowed ten-dollar hat, and she snatched it out of the air before it could hit the gravel between the rumble seat of a Packard and the front grille of a Hispano-Suiza. The near disaster brought her back to reality, although reality on this warm afternoon in May was nearly as outlandish as the mediaeval-looking Castello in front of her. Because in early April Miss Francesca Ray had been a substitute teacher for the Vancouver school board, and by mid-April she'd become an extra in the movies.

Frankie had no way of knowing what percentage of the vehicles trundling by had spent the morning parked outside studio lots, or how many passing pedestrians yearned for long hours under hot klieg lights, but it was bound to be high. And she was one of them. Frankie and thousands like her made up the bottom rung of Hollywood's complex production. Uncredited, disparaged, and only lightly paid, she and her fellow extras nevertheless appeared on film, just like movie stars.

Almost exactly like movie stars.

Gosh. Not at all like movie stars, actually, but it was a start. And today, two weeks after she'd been hired, she was fired and banned from the Monument Studios lot.

Frankie set her chums' communal ten-dollar hat, with its velvet piping and upright feather, back on her head. Twenty girls had gone without butter or coffee for a week to buy it—fifty cents apiece—and it was a pointy, up-to-date miracle of style. Better still, over the last couple of weeks, this hat had maintained a one-in-three string of successful job interviews for the young female extras who lived in Paradise Gardens Villas. This residence was slightly seedy but conveniently located next to the Garden of Allah, where movie stars swam in a turquoise pool, and across Sunset Boulevard from the famed Castello.

Trust in the hat. Frankie looked up and down the street for her best friend since childhood, Connie Mooney, who was late as usual. Connie hadn't gone shares on the hat, because her looks guaranteed employment if there was any to be had. Frankie felt in her pocket for her prop pince-nez, ready to pull out if the hotel needed secretarial help. She straightened her skirt and dived through the traffic towards her job interview.

The macadam path from Sunset Boulevard to the Castello was easy on her good shoes, and flowers scented the air above the herbaceous border. It all made a terrific first impression, but a second look revealed stringy weeds among the blossoms and mud from the downpour two days before lumped across the bottom step of the grand entry. She deduced, with undeniable relief, that the Castello manager was still looking for paid help. Sure enough, on the left-hand door of the grand Castello entrance, the *Employees Wanted, See Hotel Manager* notice still hung from its drawing pins.

Frankie had been inside the Castello foyer on one previous occasion, when she and Connie had swanned in for a rubberneck among the rich, but they had got no further than the front desk before the manager emerged from his office. His eyebrows were so bushy and his hands so red that they'd fled just in time to hide their laughter.

The hotel's knobby waiting chairs and the mahogany desk with its brass summoning bell stood now as they'd stood before, and sunlight still slanted through the tall windows on Frankie's right. But something had changed in the stuffy, proper room over the past few weeks; in fact, here were two more clues pointing to a staff shortage. The gladiolas, sitting in cloudy water on a table by the window, were brown at the tips. More telling still, the manager himself, with impatient jerks of his elbow, was running a carpet cleaner back and forth in front of the brass-plated elevator. This in a well-cut suit.

Frankie cleared her throat. "Excuse me, I think you're the manager?"

"Indeed. For my sins, the owners tell me."

She smiled at his joke. "I hope you'll consider me for a job."

"Can you garden?"

"I cannot." Frankie could, but a gardening job would be no help to the other extras or to their Queen, Loretta Desirée, who needed Frankie's eyes and ears inside the Castello with the movie stars. They all paid their rent with a combination of money earned from hotel work and gossip fed to the columnist Blanche Carver. "I can run a carpet cleaner, though, and I'm quick up the stairs with a tray."

Footsteps clattered outside the foyer. The front door banged open, and Connie rushed up to them. Her dress was buttoned wrongly up the front, and there was a snag in her right stocking. This self-patented disorder in her dress appeared accidental but in fact reliably showcased her red-headed beauty. This week alone, three other establishments had hired her with enthusiasm — and just as quickly fired her for failing to show up for her work shifts in order to act as an extra in the movies.

Connie said, "I'm here with Frankie to apply for a job."

"First this platinum blonde and now a redhead. How wonderful." The manager scowled. "Can *you* garden?"

"Good lord, no."

Frankie said, "Connie can do anything that I can do."

Connie added, "Except work that requires typing."

"Or digging."

"Also, you should know that we don't clean windows."

"You're picky for job applicants. You should know that for a decade, this hotel has served the great men and women of Hollywood. Stars, producers, visiting western and eastern royalty ... we serve them all."

"When we serve them, do they tip?" Connie asked.

The manager frowned. "Some are generous, some are eccentric, all are paying guests."

"But—"

"*Some* of them tip. And either way we give our best. If we do our job right, we are invisible."

Connie was farthest from invisible of anybody Frankie knew, but they were used to playing to each other's strengths, and Frankie was confident that she could be invisible enough for two. She said, "Are there still openings?"

"Sadly. I need chambermaids."

Frankie and Connie exchanged exultant looks.

The manager's frown deepened. "You should know that I've had to fire a pair of chambermaids for pilfering. Do you pilfer?"

"We do not pilfer," Frankie said.

"Frankie's father is a minister," Connie offered.

Frankie could have added *defrocked* to the title, but she decided not to overdo the honesty. Nobody liked a show-off.

"Can you at least make beds and clean?"

They nodded. There was only one caveat, and Frankie was about to raise the question when the manager got in first.

"And don't even think of bunking off work to be in the movies."

This sounded to Frankie like an opening to negotiations, but she clammed up at a nudge from Connie, the Paradise Gardens top expert in getting hired and fired. "Frankie would be the first to say we'd never dream of running off to the movies. We were born to be chambermaids, for we feel that the world has enough movie actresses. Right, chum?"

Frankie avoided the outright lie and folded her hands at her waist as she'd seen servants do in the movie *Love and Marie Antoinette*.

"Good. The Castello comes first in hearts and minds." The manager studied them through narrowed eyes, and Frankie wondered whether vanity prevented him from wearing the glasses tucked into his breast pocket. "Just watch your step and don't chatter at the residents. You're hired . . ."

Frankie and Connie thanked him and turned to go.

"... *if* you start right now."

"Dressed like this?" Frankie touched the marvellous pointed hat.

"Dressed in a uniform," the manager snapped. "You'll find pinnies in the ground floor janitor's closet next to the elevator."

"Pinnies? Oh, joy," Connie said. "And where doth we find our buttonhooks and sun bonnets?"

The manager shot a quelling look in Connie's direction. "Caps are on the top shelf. And both of you, cover your hair."

The janitor's closet was such a jumble of mops, brooms, and dirty dusters that Frankie cheered up and wondered whether he was really as much a hard-line boss as he sounded. She tucked her hat on the top shelf between protective boxes of soap powder while Connie pulled out two flat sateen maid's caps. These sat low on the brow and tied at the back of the head. Frankie grimaced. Maroon was not only an unfashionable colour, it was the cruellest shade in existence for redheads like Connie. However, even a colour that looked the way mothballs smelled couldn't dim Connie's good looks.

Aprons matched the caps and were unaccountably enormous. A marsupial-styled pocket below the waistbands pouched out exactly where nobody would want to pouch, and, pinned to the left breast of each, little white tags bore the names *Sylvia* and *Margery*. The two young women clapped their palms together and straightened each other's cap.

"My dear Margery, here's to a bumper crop of gossip," Frankie said.

Connie snapped a Girl Guide salute. "Sweet Sylvia, our futures are shiny with lemon wax."

"Indeed. I bags the vacuuming, Margery."

"A fair bags. Then I claim not-the-commodes, Sylvia."

The manager moved behind the reception desk and picked up the brass bell. "You two chambermaids, over here to me."

Frankie and Connie hurried to the desk. They double-looped the sashes of the all-consuming aprons and tied them in front.

The manager peered at his new hires with an obvious lack of delight. "Another pair of bright-eyed greenhorns," he sighed. "Please remember that your duty is to keep the patrons happy, the woodwork shining, and the WCs doing a steady duty. See this?" He held up the big brass bell with his thumb on the clapper so that it didn't sound. "This is the alarm bell. I'll ring it three times for emergency staff assembly in the foyer here, and ten times for fire. Now, let me tell you the regulations as communicated to me by the chief of our local fire department."

Frankie said, "Please do." The more time she and Connie spent listening to fire department regulations, the less time they would spend cleaning commodes. The manager stood with his back to the elevator and stairway while he talked, and the young women listened. They stood elbow to elbow and tried not to look up at the top of the stairs, where a young fellow in a round maroon bell-hop's cap grinned down at them. And winked. Connie smothered a laugh, and the manager turned to look. But he was too late, for the cheerful face had withdrawn from view. The manager continued his tale of correct procedures for escorting residents out of the building.

The bell-hop reappeared halfway down the stairs. And by the time the manager had taken them through procedures for counting residents and staff, he'd reached the bottom of the stairs and was revealed to be suited entirely in maroon sateen. His eyes widened in a meaningful manner. Frankie, who had taught elementary school and understood the silent language of miscreants, covered what she expected to be the bell-hop's dash for freedom by asking the manager which buckets and mops to use in washrooms. Connie, not herself a teacher but a born mischief maker, dived straight into the pretence.

As a result, the manager stood facing into the janitor's closet, explaining cleaning duties and specifying the equipment for each, while Frankie and Connie were treated to the extraordinary scene that unfolded behind his back.

The bell-hop made a swift and silent dash from the stairs to the door, and opened it to admit a second bell-hop also dressed in maroon sateen. The first was fair and several inches taller than the second. The second was swarthy and might easily be cast as a supporting pirate in the films. The two exchanged their ivory name tags, and the first bell-hop rushed out the door. The pirate bell-hop pinned the name tag to the breast of his uniform and ran for the stairs. Frankie wished she could communicate to him that his step was too heavy for stealth. Sure enough, the manager turned and caught him.

"You there," the manager said. "Come and help these young women."

"Yes, sir." The pirate bell-hop approached. His eyes gleamed and his step swaggered; his name tag was pinned crookedly in testimony to the rushed exchange with his tall, fair counterpart. It read *Jimmy*. He grinned at Frankie and Connie and touched three fingers to his forehead in a casual salute.

"Jimmy, before they start cleaning, please take these girls around and acquaint them with the layout and requirements of the job," the manager said. "Begin by repeating the Castello employee motto for Sylvia and Margery here."

The pirate bell-hop's expression grew solemn. "Sylvia and Margery, our motto is *Help the guests, remain invisible, and obey the manager.*"

This sounded uncannily similar in structure to the Boy Scout motto, and Frankie wondered if Lord Baden-Powell himself might not have been an early guest at the Castello.

"Can you repeat that, girls?"

Frankie and Connie could, did, and saluted.

The manager nodded with more weariness than Frankie thought appropriate to what was apparently meant to be a stirring moment. Still, she supposed any business that relied on young people to be servile and clean things would tire out the most enthusiastic manager. Add in the fact that the Castello catered to moneyed Hollywood folk, of whom over the past weeks Frankie had illuminating experience, and she felt a spark of compassion for her new boss. She wondered why he stayed on the job when he so clearly disliked it. Maybe, like so many here in Hollywood, he was hoping for a break in the movies; perhaps he'd been waiting for years. Sympathy for her new boss produced in Frankie an unexpected and unwished-for determination to do good work as a chambermaid, but she reminded herself that her first duties were to earn her wage, seek out gossip, and find a way back into the movies. Her loyalty was to the crowd at Paradise Gardens, and her career lay not in movie stars' WCs but in front of the movie studios' cameras.

Thus, enveloped as much in determination as in maroon sateen, Frankie followed Connie and the pirate bell-hop up to the landing above the Castello's reception hall. Here a spacious area was furnished with two leather chairs and a cloth-draped table topped with an empty flower vase. Double doors labelled 2A and 2B stood on opposite walls, each embellished with much dusty floral carving. One wall of the landing displayed a bank of small lights with brass numbers next to them, from 2A to 5D. A second stairway led up from the landing. Frankie and Connie hung over the railing and saw that the foyer below stood empty.

"The manager's in his office next to the janitor's closet. God knows what he does in there, but he only comes out about once an hour," the pirate said.

"Like a cuckoo?" Connie suggested.

"He's that, all right. I'm Cedric Bartholomew."

"Good lord, I hope not," Frankie said.

Connie said, "I'll bet last week you were Bartholomew Cedric."

"Don't you like *Cedric Bartholomew?*" The pirate scowled. "Darn. Well, I guess it was kind of a reach."

"You're no Cedric," Frankie said. "You're a swashbuckler type. How about *Robert Blackbeard?*"

The pirate cheered up. "*Davey Killerman?*"

"Or *William Kidd.* He was a real pirate, on the seven seas."

"That's the one. I'm William Kidd." He looked pleased. "It'll get me into oater movies too."

Connie obliged him with a *yippee yi yo.*

"But you should be a pirate first, because they'll be the A movies," Frankie said. "Now, Mr Kidd, tell us about this board of numbered lights."

"Aye, matey. It's numbered with each room, from luxury apartments 2A and B on this floor to the attic rooms on 5."

"And exactly what do we do when a number lights up?"

"You push the button and go to the right room, my genius girl." The pirate's new screen name had evidently gifted him with an unwelcome overconfidence, but Frankie let it pass.

"Do we go empty-handed or with some sort of chambermaid equipment?"

As if in answer, the 3A light blinked, and steps on the stairway heralded the descent of a young woman aproned and capped like Frankie and Connie. She hurried up to them, straightened her wire-rimmed glasses, and peered at the lights. Her name tag read *Edith*.

"Golly, it's 3A again. They'll want Hildy." She dipped into her apron pocket and pulled out a handful of ivory name tags. She held out a tag to Frankie, who took it between two fingers. "Now, you're Hildy."

"She's *Margery*," Connie explained. "And I'm Sylvia."

Frankie nodded. "Hello, Edith."

"For cat's sake," Edith said. "We're whatever our name tags call us. I was Hildy all week, and that's sufficient for me."

"I'm not sure about this system," Frankie said. "I feel that we should be getting credits under our own names, like in the movies."

Edith spiked her with a look. "You're an actress too, I hope?"

"We both are."

"So, the good thing about this job is that we're interchangeable, and the manager only looks at our name tags, so we can come and go freely to the studios."

"But I don't see how that would work, unless all the residents look at the name tags too."

William Kidd said, "Rich people. We're invisible, remember?"

Frankie frowned. "So how does any work get done if we're all off at the movies?"

The 3A light was still blinking, and Edith glared at it. She pinned the *Hildy* tag to Frankie's breast, took her *Margery* tag, and rattled it in with the others in her pocket. "There are twelve employee name tags. And twelve people show up to get paid. But really there are thirty of us, and we share tips and salary."

"Equally? What about the work?"

"Also equally shared," William Kidd said.

"There's no such thing," Frankie observed. "It's like higher mathematics. You can't divide work evenly. How would you keep records of who does what when?"

"We do what we can, when we can, and take an even split."

To Frankie, along with the manager's unwillingness to wear his corrective lenses, this went a long way towards explaining all the dust and dead flowers.

"But how would he know which two of you he fired for pilfering?"

"We didn't. And he doesn't. Those two still work here. And you do too. So that makes a thirty-two-way split of our salaries and tips. Therefore, we all get less."

"And everybody wants more. That's a universal constant," Frankie observed. "So Connie and I can count ourselves unpopular?"

"How unfair," Connie said.

"Sure," William Kidd said. "You didn't know what you were getting into."

Edith added, "Relax, girls, because last in gets the worst choice of chores. You get the toilets, and first call for room 3A, and the skirt chaser on four. Everybody will like you just fine for taking all that on."

Frankie and Connie exchanged a look. It was the look they'd been exchanging since first grade, and it meant *nothing's really good or bad until we get our hands on it.*

Frankie said, "Well, in that case, let's start using everybody's real or stage names from now on. No more of this Hildy, Margery, and Sylvia business."

Connie said, "I'll bet they call us all *hey, you* anyway."

"I guess we'd better run up to room 3A and see what they want. Thanks, William. Thanks, Edith."

"If we're doing real names, I'm Veronica," said she-who-was-no-longer-Edith. "And if we're doing film credit names, I'm Veronica Buckingham. I just heard there's an open call for extras for a big crowd scene at Monument Studios."

William Kidd's eyes lit up. He puckered his lips and hooted like an owl. Five maroon-clad young women stormed down the stairs and onto the landing. The door to rooms 2A and 2B opened, and two more appeared.

"Where?" the 2A woman asked.

"Keep it down, all of you. Monument Studios," Veronica Buckingham said. "And not a second to spare. I got news of the open call from a pal at the Hotel Hollywoodland, and she got it from the Ambassador. We'd better move our tail-feathers, chums."

The 2B chambermaid said, "We'll have to clap out to see who stays."

Veronica Buckingham grinned. "Meet the new kids. They'll hold the fort. Keep a lookout, you."

William Kidd leaned over the railing to keep watch while, with practised movements, the young people whipped off hats and aprons and tossed them to Frankie and Connie. Now on tiptoe, the group of extras hurried down the stairs.

Frankie juggled her armful of maroon sateen uniforms. "Connie, you'd better go as well."

"What, and leave you playing Cinderella? You're coming too."

"I can't. I've been banned from Monument Studios."

Connie stared. "How'd you manage that?"

"The assistant director didn't like a suggestion I made about giving close-ups to the extras."

"What a good idea. Anyone ought to grasp the benefits."

"There's nothing good about an idea that gets a person kicked out of the studios."

"But not blackballed."

"Maybe blackballed."

Connie shook her head. "I'll stay."

The light over 3A was still blinking. "Give me the caps and aprons and go. I'd go if it was you who'd got barred."

"No, you wouldn't."

"Sure, I would. We've got to keep the ball rolling if we want to get ahead in this business. Go on, be in a movie. Be in two."

Connie handed her armful of maroon sateen to Frankie, took off her own cap and apron, and set them on top of the pile. "I'll do it for us."

"*Abso-tively.*"

"*Posi-lutely.*"

Connie saluted Frankie and ran down the stairs.

Alone on the landing, Frankie peered around for somewhere to hide the bundled uniforms and settled on the small table between the armchairs. She stuffed the hats and uniforms under the table and draped the cloth to hide the bulge. Satisfied, she pushed the button by the blinking light and ran for the stairs up towards Room 3A.

Frankie was twenty-two, or eighteen in Hollywood years, and while she had little experience in the movies,* she had years of practice back home in Vancouver, asking her unreasonably bedridden father what he wanted and getting it for him without losing her natural high spirits or hopes for the future. She doubted whether any of the Castello residents could challenge her more severely than had Sheridan D Ray, defrocked minister and author of several leather-bound collections of sermons which, when thrown towards Frankie across his bedroom, landed on the floor with a hell-like thunder.

So Frankie had a geometrical understanding of which way to duck when something was thrown at her. What was more, she knew how to make up a bed. All in all, Frankie was up to her new job as a Castello Hotel chambermaid. She had to be smart and swift; around skirt-chasing residents she would be wise to keep a clear line to the door. But she could never forget that making beds and gathering gossip were only means to an end. Success in chambermaiding was not her goal: she was an actress.

She rounded the corner of the stairway, and her steps tapped out the rhythm of her new life in Hollywood. Look and listen. And watch for any chance or connection that would help her get back into the movies where she belonged. Who knew what opportunities awaited a can-do young woman at the famous Castello Hotel? She was convinced that good luck abounded in Hollywood, even though setbacks heralded success. And was there ever a worse setback than being blackballed by King Samson, the cantankerous producer and head of Monument Studios? Two weeks previously, she had nearly been killed in an

---

* See *The Extra*, Book 1 of the Monument Studios Mysteries.

on-set fire there, but she'd survived, and she trusted that dangers like that were behind her. Now the worry was only that she'd lose her acting chops.

It was not enough to do good work as a chambermaid. She must play the role to the hilt. King Samson and Monument Studios had fired her, but they couldn't stop her from acting.

Frankie hurried up to the third-floor landing and, in character, rapped twice on the nearest apartment door. A flutter of piano notes from somewhere nearby augured well for the scene. She stood with her hands folded before her, ready for the door to Room 3A to open. But a second glance showed her that she'd knocked at Room 3C by mistake and, furthermore, that each door was equipped with its own bell. She crossed the landing and rang the correct doorbell.

Inside Room 3A, the piano music trailed off with a flourish and footsteps sounded. The door opened inward, and there in the opening, in shirtsleeves, braces, and flannel trousers, stood the highest-paid movie director in the business. Frankie's heart leaped. She dropped all pretence at playing a chambermaid and stood tall in her maroon uniform, as if the horrible apparel had nothing to do with her at all.

"I hope I can be of help, Mr McMann," she said.

The famed director's eyes lit up. "You're new. And I like you already. What's your name?"

Des McMann smelled of aftershave, hard liquor, and typewriter ribbons. Further, he beamed at Frankie like a good-looking young uncle at a favourite niece. Here was a man who operated at the top of the Hollywood establishment; she marvelled at his apparent humanity. *You're new. I like you.* These were not words a hopeful extra expected to hear from a Hollywood director. In fact, the directorial phrases *Hurry up, damn you* and, in Frankie's case, *Get off my set and stay off* still resonated. She wondered how best to answer the director. Waxing humble was out of character for the proud bearing she'd assumed. She could easily match his hail-fellow-well-met enthusiasm with some of her own, but that was poor drama. With only a moment to think, she settled on a warm and quiet dignity, like Greta Garbo but without the Swedish accent.

She inclined her head. "Mr McMann, what a pleasure to meet you. I am new, and I'm here to help."

"You know," he said, "I rang the bell because I was hoping that somebody would——"

The door to Room 3C slammed open. Frankie and the director turned, and in the doorway, fists on hips, stood King Samson, producer and head of Monument Studios, the studio which had that very day cast Frankie from its gates and onto Sunset Boulevard, alone——except for her friends——and unemployed——except for this job. The worst of it was that she and Samson had faced off more than once under difficult circumstances. Her only hope lay in King Samson's often-repeated boast that he never remembered the little people.

King Samson said, "McMann, did you knock on my door and run off?"

Frankie said, "I ..."

Des McMann touched Frankie's arm. So directed, she fell silent.

He said, "Sorry, Samson. In my defence, there's a mischievous child in each of us if we feed it with fun."

King Samson scowled. "I'll kick your behind if you play that trick again."

"I think you should, absolutely." To Frankie, Des McMann added, "Young woman, please restrain me if I knock and run again. Hold on to my braces, then let them snap. That'll teach me."

King Samson narrowed his gaze. "McMann, I don't like you."

"I like you," McMann said. "I like everybody."

"And you'll burn in Hell for it," Samson said. "I can only hope that I'm down there too so I can watch you sizzle."

King Samson slammed the door. Frankie exchanged a wide-eyed look with McMann, and from his expression she was as certain as dogs love dirt that he was about to burst out laughing. Before he could, the door to Room 3C slammed back open, and King Samson loomed again, drawing breath. Frankie moved a little closer to McMann, as one might take shelter from a storm beneath a sturdy tree.

King Samson said, "McMann, I loathe everything you stand for in the business of making movies. Do you know why? Because I work for my successes. I keep my directors on script and off creative invention. I keep my writers creative and pay them less than everybody except the extras so that they'll burst their hearts to turn out the best screenplays in the shortest time. I find vain, talented actors and bend them into shapes they've never made before on the screen. And what do you do?"

"I don't do that," McMann said.

"I know you don't. Here's what you do." Samson shoved his hands deep into his pockets and leaned towards Frankie and McMann. "You play the piano. You get folks in the mood. You gentle them like ponies and encourage their tiny minds to think up some lines they'd like to say. You send them out for liquid lunches and walk around in circles until something comes to you. You're a highly paid amateur walking the edge of chaos. And you'll fall, McMann. You'll fall hard. To the bottom of the barrel."

The bottom of the barrel. Today of all days, Samson's words sounded worse than a tirade. They might have been a curse delivered with power and fury upon McMann's head. Frankie wondered exactly how an apparently kind man at the top of his field would answer King Samson's tirade.

McMann laughed. He said, "You've hit the nail with your hammer there, Sammy. It's not the last time I'll hear it, and it's certainly not the first. Even long ago, when I was beginning behind the camera back in '22, I heard it from a man who lived and died in this very Castello not so long ago. A man we've not heard of since, although he was once as great as you and me. No, greater, because we learned from him. He created the sense and shape of what we do. He formed filmmaking whole, like Prometheus in a pork-pie hat, out of the mud of inspiration."

Frankie had made a serious study of hundreds of movie magazine articles, and she now searched her memory for the one man that the best director in the world said was better than he. Zodor? Gleason? Tremblay?

"Forrest!" King Samson barked the name. "All the old master did was get his hands on a camera when we were still buckling our pants at our knees, McMann. All he did was get there first."

McMann nodded. "He made the *there* here."

Samson said, "And he wrote the perfect screenplay."

"Which one?" Frankie dared ask, in case she ever had a chance to be in it.

Des McMann said, "No one knows. That's the beauty of it."

King Samson said, "That's the hell of it. I'd pay a bundle to get my hands on it." He turned his gaze to Frankie. "I know you."

"No, you don't," Frankie said, "*sir*. I'm just the chambermaid."

"Hmph. I know you, and I'll bet I don't like you either. But you're a maid, and I'll tell you what I tell all the maids. I'll pay you twenty dollars if you find that screenplay."

"I'm not a maid, I'm a chambermaid," Frankie said stoutly. "And as for twenty dollars …"

McMann made a calming gesture with his hands. "It's called the Lost Screenplay because it's lost, Samson. Forrest even told me it was lost."

"McMann, you were born under a lucky moon, but you're a lunatic. Whatever insult Forrest slung at you back in the day, it slings double from me." Samson paused a beat. "What did he say to you, anyway? Did he let you in on any of his thinking on story? I'd be pretty interested to know."

Frankie was agog to know how McMann would answer Samson, and also to learn some of GX Forrest's filmmaking secrets. But she was not to make either discovery that morning, for somewhere beneath them a bell rang—and kept on ringing in triple soundings separated by a second's pause.

"To hell with bells," Samson said.

"Is that the fire alarm? I'd better save the vodka if it is," McMann said. "And also the good half of the movie treatment I'm working on."

"I've got a desk covered in god-awful movie treatments, and they can all burn along with their authors," Samson said. "Grab your screenplay, and let's go down and see what's on fire."

Frankie had been trying to recall the details of the Castello manager's bell-ringing lecture, and now she spoke up. "Fire is ten rings, sir. That's only three rings. It's a call to staff to gather in the foyer."

"Staff! What's that infernal noise doing in my ears if it's meant for staff? Unbelievably poor service." King Samson glared at McMann, stepped back inside his apartment, and slammed the door behind him.

McMann laughed again. "Well, my dear, you'd better hurry along to the foyer with the rest of them."

"Yes, sir." Frankie blinked. Her maroon sateen cap felt tight across her brow. There was no *rest of them*. They were all off being extras, leaving Frankie the only acting member of staff in the Castello. And if she alone answered the bell, the jig would be up for the lot of them. Everybody would be fired, or at least forced to work traditional hours as hotel staff only. What a mournful end that would be to the perfect extra's setup on her first day at work.

"What's wrong?" McMann frowned. "For heaven's sake, is the manager going on about theft in the Castello again?"

"He must be," Frankie said.

McMann glanced upwards, and at the stairway, and back to Frankie. "I take it you're the only one here? The rest of the kids are working at the studios?"

Frankie let out a breath. McMann knew. "There's only me."

"So if the manager is looking for a thief, he'll accuse you?"

She hadn't thought of that. "And I won't be able to deny it."

"But you didn't steal anything, you honest young part-time chambermaid. Oh! I see." McMann sighed. "You can't say it wasn't you because you'd be putting your co-workers up for the crime."

"And …"

"And assuring the discovery of their harmless efforts at career advancement when they're meant to be cleaning the toilets here. Well, come on. And, one more thing, sweet chambermaid—"

She shook her head. No more servant names. "Frankie."

"Really? I like that. *Frankie.* One more thing, Frankie. In order that we movie folk can create the best scene possible, you and I must make a lot of noise going down the stairs. We will try to sound like all the members of the Castello staff together. Now, cue the thunder of many feet descending."

Frankie thundered.

There was no mistaking the look in the manager's eye. It communicated a fierce exasperation. She'd expected no less; what she had not foreseen was that Des McMann would stop at the first-floor landing to play the challenging role of a dozen people clumping about and giggling.

Frankie took the last set of stairs solo and, with only her faith in a director she'd just met and her shield of nearly complete innocence to protect her, stood before the manager. She straightened her apron and clasped her hands.

"Am I the first one here, sir?"

The manager looked along his nose at her. "Indeed. I wonder what that means in the big picture of criminal enterprise. Did you know there would be a theft? Did you know it because you committed it?"

"I did not, sir. Exactly what was stolen, and from whom?"

"I will tell you when all the suspects have descended." The manager peered at her apron bib. "Where's your name tag? You must always wear your name tag."

"Yes, sir."

"Where is it, then?"

"I don't know, sir. I can tell you it said my name was Margery."

"Did you take your name tag off because you would not be identified by Mrs Forrest if she caught you stealing, Margery?"

"Certainly not, sir." The manager's inquisition was clearly aimed to unsettle, but it was so like the questioning she and Connie had experienced when they were up to their tricks as children that it relaxed her instead. "I haven't met Mrs Forrest. Which apartment is hers?"

"Her is 5C," the manager said. "But I'm investigating here. Now, think hard. Have any of the other members of staff recently seemed to have more money than they should?"

Frankie scorned to remind him that she'd come on staff only half an hour before. She said, "No, sir."

"Are you certain? Perhaps one of them is wearing new Italian shoes or a silk frock?"

Frankie shook her head. She wanted to point out that the manager was sporting the only expensive-looking clothing of any staff member she'd met. She was beginning to feel less worried about her continued employment at the Castello and more indignant at the manager's apparently baseless accusations of his juniors on staff.

She knew she oughtn't to say it. But she said it. "Anyway, sir, why are you so sure the thief is one of us?"

"Bravo!" Des McMann's cheer sounded from the stairs. "*Ecce veritas*, sir."

"*Hic est veritas*," Frankie corrected him, for she was, after all, a schoolmarm and the daughter of a cleric.

"*Hic, hec, hoc*," McMann offered, getting it right this time. He moved quickly down the last stairway to the foyer. "Get ready, Mr Manager, because I'm coming down and I'm on a high horse."

"*Equus*," the manager said coldly.

"And to you, too." McMann took the manager's hand and shook it. "Frankie here has *rem acu tetigisti*. Which means, dear girl …?"

"It means *touched the matter with a needle*; that is to say, I'm exactly right."

McMann said, "*Hic est* indeed *veritas*. And with that we leave ancient languages behind us and proceed to the truth before us now. There is no reason to believe that these recent thefts were committed by your young staff members. I believe you've fired every one of them you suspected …"

"Except this one," the manager pointed out.

"And still the thefts continue. So why couldn't it be a cat burglar, in through the window and out with the loot?"

"Unlikely," the manager said. "For how would the thief case the Castello? How would he know what to steal?"

McMann nodded. "*Rem acu tetigisti.*"

"You did say no more Latin," Frankie reminded the director.

"I did. Now tell me why, sir, the thief could not be one of the residents of the Castello?"

Before the manager could answer, the front door slammed open, and a workman ran in. "Fire," he said.

"No, it's three bells to summon the staff," the manager corrected him.

"There's no smoke with summoning," the workman said. "Come and see."

The manager snatched up his bell, and McMann, the manager, and Frankie followed the workman outside to see smoke wafting up from the upper stories of the Castello. Frankie craned her head to see from exactly where the smoke emanated, while the manager rang the bell.

Anybody, such as Frankie, who came from a city of wood-framed houses, like Vancouver, would recognize that beneath the exterior stucco of the Castello was a wood-frame building in a dry climate.

"Fire on the top floor!" the manager cried. "Get upstairs, Margery."

"I think you'll want a fireman," McMann mused. "If you spend money on specialists, I think you'll find it's worth the expense."

"Margery will do her job, and I'll do mine, which is to wait outside for the fire trucks. You go back inside and call the fire station, and this fellow here"—he nodded at the workman— "can begin filling buckets to throw upon the flames."

"No, I'll call the fire department," the workman said. "And then I'll get some friends over here, but you'll have to pay us if you want us to sling buckets."

"Invoice the hotel, please. Margery, begin with the apartments on the first floor. Knock on every door and get our guests out to safety. Alert the rest of the staff to work upwards to empty the building."

Frankie and McMann exchanged a glance. There was no other staff to call; nor was there means to recall the porters and chambermaids from the studios.

The manager rang the fire bell. Frankie ran with McMann into reception, past the workman at the telephone, and up the stairs to the landing. The two hammered on the doors of rooms 2A and 2B.

A woman in a robe ran out of Room 2A, and Frankie recalled her fire drill experience as a substitute teacher.

"Are your doors and windows shut tight?" she asked.

"*Va au diable*," the woman answered, and hurried down the stairs.

Des McMann translated. "That means *go to the devil*."

"Thanks, Mr McMann, but I taught French. You should get to safety with the other guests."

"I'll tell you what." McMann rolled back his shirtsleeves then removed his tie and tucked it in his pants pocket. "I haven't once knocked on doors and run this week. Let's pretend it's April Fool's Day. Lead the way, Frankie."

"The manager said to start on the lower floors and work up, but the fire's on the top floor."

"That's because the rich guests are on the lower floors and the poor are up top. Usually in Hollywood you can expect to start at the bottom, but in this case …"

"The top it is. We'll run up and call out as we go."

"You'll call out. I'll save my breath for running and for carrying elderly guests to safety, until I die a hero's death, overcome by smoke amid falling beams and flying sparks."

Frankie had lately escaped just such a near-fatal incendiary, and she scurried up the stairs to the next floor and the next, shouting, "Fire!" as she went. By the third floor, McMann's pace had flagged, and when Frankie reached the top floor, his footsteps sounded on the stairs a floor below.

The stairs ended here, at the attic landing. Four closed doors stood before her, and stencilled numbers read *5A* through *5D* at the top; the bottoms of the doors were chipped and scuffed. To her left, a closet-sized storage space was jammed with wooden crates and newspapers, crisp at the edges. Once the fire caught here, nothing would stop it from consuming the Castello from the top down, the way a shark devoured a swimmer.

Or did sharks eat one's feet first?

Frankie shook her head and pulled herself together as Des McMann trudged up the last few stairs to arrive at her side. Together they hammered on the four doors. There was no answer at 5D, 5C, or 5B; but out of 5A a voice called, "Cuckoo!"

The door opened, and before them stood an elderly woman, delicately drawn in silver and ashes of roses. Black smoke wafted out of the short corridor at her back.

"Hello, Gillian," McMann said. "You never age a day, do you?"

"Sweet Dester McMann," Gillian replied. "Always the loveliest of boys."

Frankie said, "I'm sorry to say that the Castello is on fire, ma'am. You must come out."

"Come in," the woman answered. "I was about to pour sherry for us all."

She turned and disappeared through the smoke, back inside her apartment.

Frankie looked at Des McMann, not so much for guidance as to judge whether he'd recovered sufficiently from his four-storey climb to help carry the woman down the stairs. "Are there more people in her apartment, do you think?"

"I can only rescue one." McMann placed his hands on his hips, wiped the sweat from his brow, and looked ready to overpower the old lady for her own good. "And only a little one, mind, like Gillian. If you herd out the other sherry drinkers, we can chase ourselves down the stairs and outside in an eye-blink. I'll bring the sherry."

"Gillian!" Frankie called into the smoky corridor.

Gillian reappeared. "Would you prefer a little hot whiskey? That's what GX is taking. Good for the liver. Follow me, everyone."

Frankie was aware that GX Forrest had passed from this world some years before. Still, there was nothing for it but to ignore her fears and follow Gillian into the smoke.

Frankie took off her cap and fanned the smoke away from her face. The fug thickened as she moved deeper into Gillian Forrest's rooms. Beneath her maroon apron's bib, panic rose in her breast, and she recognized the truth of the old adage, *The burned child fears the fire.* She wanted nothing more than to tear out of the apartment, down the stairs, and out the doors into the clean Los Angeles air. But an old lady and the world's greatest movie director were walking into danger.

She followed Gillian Forrest and Des McMann into a dining room where black smoke billowed along the ceiling above an oval pedestal table. In the centre of the table, a large brass bowl held a mass of uncoiled film and bunched-up paper, all of it burning with less flame, and more smoke and stink, than Frankie would have believed possible from a tabletop fire.

She rushed to the open window and heard sirens; she could only faintly make out the Castello garden below. Inspiration struck, and satisfaction followed: she pulled off her heavy, oversized apron and flung it over the burning bowl.

She asked, "Mrs Forrest, why are you burning reels of film?"

Gillian Forrest frowned at the apron bunched on her tabletop. "GX asked me to burn some reels of film."

Frankie and McMann exchanged glances. She didn't have to be told to step carefully with Forrest's widow. The old woman looked as if a gust of wind from the open window might blow her off her feet, straight up to Heaven to be with GX.

"Why, Gillian?" McMann asked gently. "Why would GX

want to burn his own films? His own brilliant oeuvre?"

"Not his oeuvre, silly boy. One of his rivals' films. He buys them and he burns them. Or sometimes he unwinds the reels at the dump."

GX Forrest was long past unwinding film at the dump, but Frankie said nothing. And she was glad she'd kept her peace, because a door on the far side of the dining room opened, and a strongly built white-haired man stepped through it.

"GX!" Des McMann cried. "Dear man, I thought you were—"

"Asleep? So I was. And you've wakened me. Damn you to hell, you young pup. Where's the screenplay you stole from me?"

"I didn't steal it," McMann protested. "I'm the last man in Hollywood to do such a thing."

"Screenplay?" Frankie looked from McMann to the Forrests. Could GX Forrest, apparently back from the dead, be talking about the perfect Lost Screenplay? What if the Lost Screenplay was not lost at all? Somebody might find it and produce it.

A flash, like the brightest klieg lighting in the movie business, lit Frankie up inside. For Frankie might find GX Forrest's screenplay, and McMann might produce it. And what that might mean for her, Connie, and the extras at Paradise Gardens was worth dreaming about.

And acting upon.

§

For more Hollywood adventures with Frankie, pick up a copy of The Extra: A Monument Studios Mystery *by Mel Anastasiou, available from Pulp Literature Press and most bookstores.*

CHARDI KALA FOR THE MODERN DIRTBAG

Kiran K Basra

Kiran K Basra *is a neuroscience student at the University of Toronto and is a creative director at the Innis Herald. When she isn't reading and writing about children of immigrants, mean lesbians, or portals to other worlds, she is napping on the subway.*

© 2025, Kiran K Basra

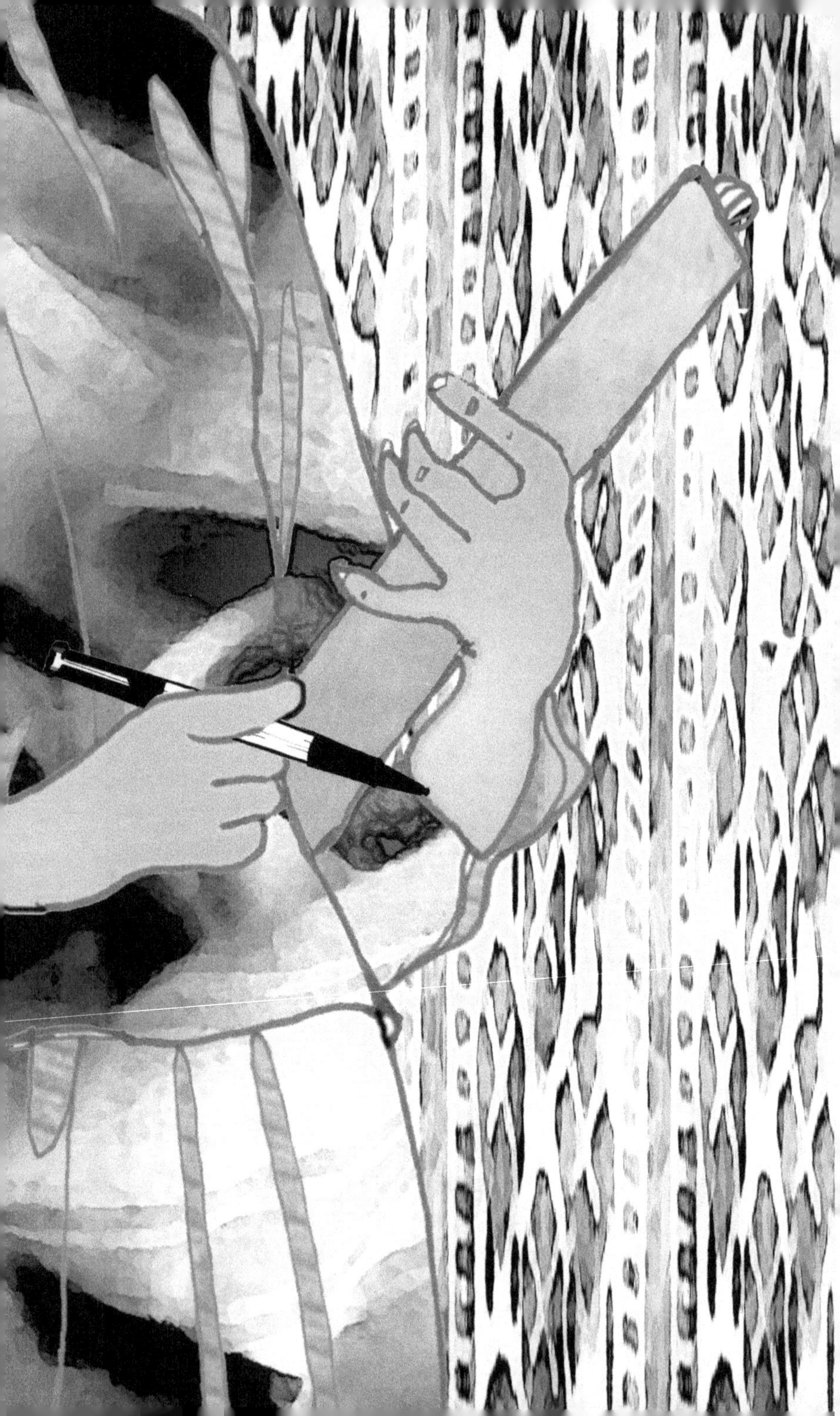

Chardi Kala for the Modern Dirtbag

Veer comes into the seniors' centre half an hour late, completely unprepared and suspecting she might still be a little high. She regrets it when she sees the pretty Filipina girl behind the desk: a ring on every finger, a patterned button-down, short hair dyed blue. There's a ninety-percent chance she's bisexual, and Veer's blown her chance before she even realized she had one. She resigns herself to a night on Hinge, leans her elbows on the counter, glances at the girl's name tag (and her tits) and says, "Hey, Reyna, I'm the mind-reader here for Roop Grewal."

"You're half an hour late. We assumed the province was just lying when they said they sent someone," Reyna says, searching for a file on her desk. She freezes. "Wait, how did you know my name? Did you—"

"Relax, gorgeous," Veer says, plucking the file out of her grasp. "It's on your name tag."

"Oh," Reyna says, as Veer strides past the desk towards room 115—the number is Sharpied onto the cover of Mrs Grewal's file. "Wait, don't we have to brief you or something? Sorry, I've never had to deal with an Eclipsed coming to work on a patient before. I don't really know how this works. Should I be saying 'someone Eclipsed' instead? I heard it's an adjective not a noun these days …"

"You're doing great," Veer says, both because the aforementioned tits are really nice and because she's trying to charm Reyna into not reporting her late and unprepared. "What happens is I go sit in Mrs Grewal's room, I hold her hand and see what I can find out about why …" She takes a moment to look at the file and see what she was supposed to do. "She stopped responding to nurses. Damn, six months ago? And the province hasn't sent anyone?"

"You didn't read the file before coming?" Reyna says. "Her brain scans are normal besides the Parkinson's, and she eats what we put in front of her and pees when we walk her to the washroom, but she doesn't say a word. She doesn't even look at you, just through you."

"Huh," Veer says, because most of her job is finding out whether people having psychotic breaks have families to go back to, or communicating for people incapable of speech or signing. She's got no idea how to approach this. "Well, I'll take a look, see what she's dreaming about and if she remembers what triggered this."

"I heard some Eclipsed see everything you've ever thought. Can you do that?"

"I don't like to without permission," Veer lies. Consent is sexy or whatever, but Veer barely has enough magic to qualify for this job. If she'd been even an hour more patient in the womb, she'd have been born right in totality, when the moon blocked the sun and the babies born could change the world. Instead, she rushed into life like she rushed into an undercut back in tenth grade, and she's ended up a support worker who can't even afford a Brampton basement apartment. She gives her best yeah-I'll-be-a-mistake-but-it'll-be-fun grin. "But if you want, I'll do a trick for you later."

She pushes her way into the room and finds a small Punjabi woman in her eighties lying under the covers of a twin bed. Someone's put her hands on her belly. She would look like a corpse if she wasn't blinking. Her *kesh*-long grey hair is spread fan-like across the pillow. It's kind of freaky—Veer has never seen a Punjabi lady her age with her hair loose. She's got a weird protective urge to braid it up, to find her earrings and bangles and put them back on her. What sort of a dick leaves their mom in an old folks' home and lets the nurses dress her like she's white?

If Reyna is still watching, she'll help Mrs Grewal after she figures out what's wrong. Girls love when people take care of kids—it's an evolutionary thing, Veer thinks, though she didn't pay much attention in bio—and maybe old people get points too?

"Aight," Veer says. She dumps her hoodie at the foot of the bed, stretches so that her T-shirt pulls tight across her chest and her mediocre biceps are flexed, plants her hand on Mrs Grewal's, and starts to tune into her mind—before something rips her off her feet and sends her flying into white space.

Foreign memories hit her like someone put her head directly in front of a tennis ball launcher. Mustard fields—the smell of a dirt road—children arguing—forcing bangles onto her wrist—fresh paratha—the sputtering of boiling oil—a man's unfamiliar breathing—new stretch marks—monsoon rain—Veer screams under the force of it all.

And as suddenly as it started, it stops. She's on her knees in a cramped kitchen, and in front of her is a woman in her thirties with the plentiful jewellery and plain shalwar kameez of a farmer's wife who's never left the village. "Who the hell are you?"

"Oh, fuck," Veer says, head aching as she tries to get her bearings. Veer has heard that good telepaths can wander through someone's mind like it's a library, but she's a terrible telepath. She knows this place doesn't exist in the world — the analogue clock on the wall is ticking but the second hand doesn't move — but she doesn't know if, when she leaves this dream, the things that happen in it will come out with her. "Am I in your head? You're Clipped, too? Fuck, you must be near totality. She should have fuckin' warned me before I — "

The woman walks closer and grabs her by the hair, pulling her face up. Veer cries out and tries to detach the hand, but Mrs Grewal has woven her fingers through the root of her braid, and her head is sending out spikes of pain with her heartbeat. She doesn't even know if it's her real body hurting or just a dream of a body. Veer is not handling this whole thing well. In fact, Veer is *losing her shit.*

"Manveer Kaur Sidhu, twenty-three years old, family from Ludhiana, born in Toronto, a homosexual, a disappointment to your parents, a womanizer, a drug addict, a university drop-out," Mrs Grewal says, letting go of her hair so that Veer has to catch herself to avoid slamming her head into the floor. Her voice echoes in that strange way that languages travel through thought. "Living paycheque to paycheque, party to party, woman to woman. No ambitions, no accomplishments. Ugly, unkind, and stupid."

"That's not nice," Veer says stupidly, struggling to her feet and trying to get her mind functioning again. "And you can't get addicted to weed. Look, can you just come back to your body? People are getting worried."

"Who?" Mrs Grewal says. "The nurses?"

"You must have family," Veer says, though if she had, they would be a lot more concerned about a woman who hasn't spoken in six months. And they wouldn't let someone dress her like that.

"Manveer, I can take over the bodies and see all the memories of anyone who looks into my eyes. Do you honestly think my children still speak to me?"

"You can make friends?"

"In this shaking body, where my English comes out twisted and no one understands my Punjabi?"

"Okay, fine," Veer says, tired of the stubbornness of old women who have decided the rest of their lives will be miserable and refuse to hear any arguments to the contrary. "If you want to wander around your own memories until your body shuts down and kills you, be my fuckin' guest. But I like my life in the world. Can you at least put me back in my body?"

"Your body's empty?" Mrs Grewal says. A terrible idea crosses her face, and Veer's stomach drops all the way out of her.

"Don't even think about it, bitch!" Veer shouts, lunging forwards. The kitchen dissolves around her and re-forms into a small closet. Before she can breathe, she's being pressed in by the walls and surrounded by layers upon layers of winter coats.

She sits cross-legged on the floor and says plaintively, "What the *fuck.*"

This is the front closet back home. Veer knows it intimately; it was the family time-out spot, and Veer had spent a lot of time sitting here in the dark thinking about what she'd done. It was an extremely effective punishment, not because she was scared of the dark—she and her brother Jodh played Narnia in here all the time—but because it was so deeply boring. Veer shoves herself against the door, waiting to spill out into the front hallway, but it's solid and unmoving. She stands up and tries harder, hammering on it and backing up into the coats to throw her shoulder against it. Nothing.

"Help!" she cries, even though this must be her own memory—there's no one here but her and the person who trapped her. "Mrs Grewal, help. You can't just leave me here. How long are you going to leave me here?"

Is Mrs Grewal still in her own mind, or is she inside of Veer? She's so frightened at the idea of someone else seeing from her eyes that she ignores the inherent dirty joke. Is she planning to go home, to be the Manveer her family gave up on a long time ago? Is she planning to start a new life, and her family will never know what happened to her? She stumbles through the *Ik Onkar* to calm herself down but can't get further than *nirbhau, nirvair.* Whenever someone quizzed her at gurdwara Sunday school, she'd just brush the wrist of whoever was closest and leach the answers from them. Now she doesn't even have God with her, just her *dadi* in the back of her head telling her to do *chardi kala* every time she complains.

She screams—wordless, high-pitched and girlish, in a way she doesn't normally let herself sound. She screams until her voice breaks in her throat, and nothing happens.

Then she wipes the sweat and snot off her face, says, "Fuck this," and gets up.

"This is my mind," she says. "You hear me, Roop?" It feels, strangely, more disrespectful to call Mrs Grewal by her first name than to call her a bitch. "Think you can work this thing better than me? No way."

Veer's powers are so much weaker than Roop's. She can press her ear against the door of someone's mind, but Roop can walk inside and take over the whole damn house. Still, she knows something about the twisted logic that governs them. She steps through the crush of winter jackets without fear, remembering Jodh at her six-year-old shoulder, believing him wholeheartedly. She walks through the crush of coats for far longer than she should be able to, and emerges into bright light.

She's back in the waiting room, her hand still clutching Roop's wrist. She tries to let go but can't, and she feels tension in her body she didn't put there — because Roop is here, making her dance like a puppet on strings. She can see what's happening, but she can't even move her own eyes to look around. If Veer thought the mindscape was bad, this is worse. Horrifyingly, she feels her mouth curve into a smile without her permission.

"I didn't expect that," her own voice says in Punjabi. "You're clumsy and weak, but I guess being stubborn makes up for it."

"What's going on?" Reyna says. "Is that like a spell or something?"

"Don't worry," her voice says in English, but it comes out different, dyed with Punjab instead of Toronto. Veer tries to thrash, to break the spell on her, but all that happens is a faint twitch of the fingers on her left hand. "I'm almost done with this. I'll make my report and someone else will come in next week."

Reyna doesn't notice the change in her voice. Veer tries to look at her, but she can't even move her own eyes. As fast as she can, before Roop can grab control of her arm again, she balls her left hand into a fist and hits herself in the sternum: *thump, thump-thump, thump-thump. This body is mine!*

"Oh, that's cool. Does the sound help somehow? Should I do that too?" Reyna asks. Her interest is very flattering — Veer loves when people pay attention to her—but it is also deeply distracting when Roop is trying to seize control of that arm again. It trembles on her chest from the force of her trying to keep it there and Roop trying to move it back, like arm-wrestling.

In the background, Reyna claps her hands together in the same pattern. "Am I doing it right?"

"It's not going to work," her voice says in Punjabi. "I've been doing this for six months, jumping from person to person. Some of them have taken control, but I always take it back. I like this body. I could use it for a long time. I could kill you and take it all for myself, I think. I never have before, but if you make me angry enough, I'll find a way."

"You know, it's not very polite to ignore someone when they're speaking to you," Reyna says, still clapping. But Veer has been thinking about action movies, when they blow up the base and then the bad guy never bothers them again. If Roop is in her mind, can Veer go into hers?

She stops trying to control her arm, and it snaps back to a neutral position so fast it yanks her elbow. Roop says, "Given up?"

Her mouth is relaxed. Roop is letting her speak, taunting her. It makes Veer fucking furious. "Yeah, not quite," she says in English, letting her Toronto accent thicken. "Fucking up my life is my job, *bhenchod*. Keep doing it, and I'll ruin yours."

She clenches her jaw and eyes shut, her whole body tensing like a rocket about to blast off. While Roop is trying to wrest control back from her, she searches through the old woman's memories and traces them back to their source. Veer follows mustard fields and boiling oil, plane rides holding fussing children, uncomfortable high-heeled shoes, twisting bitterness, useless rage, and profound loneliness. It isn't like getting swept up in a rip tide; it's like walking a tightrope, tracking ghost sensations and memories until she's left her mind and landed back in the kitchen where Roop spent the better part of her adult life.

Roop appears almost instantly. She still looks thirty-five, not like an old lady. "You? How?"

Veer is pissed. So she lets out a scream, charges, body-checks Roop to the tiled floor, and is about to get down and start punching when something catches her around the neck and starts to cut off her air. Veer stumbles back against the fridge without even the breath to scream, and Roop floats up from the floor like she's a comic book villain. Her *chunni* flutters behind her like a cape. What a Bollywood-obsessed drama queen.

"I propose a trade," Roop says, sitting on an ornate chair that has instantly appeared as Veer chokes at her feet. The pressure at her throat relieves. "You want me in the real world? You want my body useful again? I'll give you both of those. You stay here. I take you."

"What?" Veer croaks.

"It's a generous offer," Roop says. "I could always kill you."

"You *are*," Veer says, struggling to her knees. Tears drip down her cheeks.

"No, I'm sacrificing you. No one likes you, you do nothing, you're nobody at all. I waited so long to have my own life, and then I lost my own body. I was a good daughter, good sister, good wife, good mother. I deserve this!" Roop leans forward, and her eyes are hard and cold and merciless. "Give me one good reason to spare your life. What makes you deserve everything you have and waste?"

"Deserve it?" Veer says. She's so confused she stops scrubbing at her face and just stares. "That's such bullshit. I have to, what, convince you I'm worthy of the right to live? I have to make you feel better for murdering me when you decide I didn't earn my body?"

Veer sets her jaw, straightens her spine, and stands. Roop's head tilts up to watch as she plants her feet and balls her hands into fists at her side. She doesn't care if Roop thinks she's nobody. Doesn't care if Roop decides a stoned dropout dyke has no right to live to begin with. *Nirbhau, nirvair*—if she has never been a good Sikh before, if every time she's been a careless, selfish idiot has cancelled out her good, it doesn't matter. In this moment, she *is* without fear, without hatred, unbowed and undespairing.

"What are you doing?" Roop asks. "Stop that."

"*Chardi kala*," she says, and though her hands shake, her voice doesn't. She adds, belatedly, "Bitch."

And though she intends to meet death with her eyes open, she flinches when Roop makes a minute movement—and opens her eyes to find herself back in her body in the nursing home, collapsed on the floor with Reyna crouched over her and taking her pulse in her neck. She opens her mouth to make a joke, but just croaks out, "Hi."

"Oh my God, I thought the coma was contagious," Reyna says, standing. Veer doesn't even think about the loss of cool fingers on her neck, because she's back in her body, lying on the floor with her hoodie balled up under her head, and she has full control of the whole damn thing.

"Fuck, yes!" she cries, sitting up and wiggling all of her body at once, just for the sheer joy of movement. She kicks her legs, full of pins and needles, does a bhangra shoulder shrug, and kisses her own forearm with a loud smacking sound that prompts a little incredulous laugh from Reyna.

"Look, I just got possessed," she says, accepting Reyna's hand up and stumbling on her numb legs. Reyna catches her at the elbow, steadying her. Her hair smells like vanilla. "If you'd almost spent the rest of your life stuck as a grandmother, you'd be grateful too."

"Possessed? Is that why you were being so weird? Does that normally happen?" Reyna cries.

"If it did, I would not be in this line of work," Veer admits. She looks over at Roop, who is staring at the ceiling. Veer would almost think she wasn't in her body were it not for the tears dripping through her wrinkles and into her hair. "And it's not happening to nobody ever again, right?"

Roop shifts her eyes over and gives the minutest of nods.

"If you didn't give consent, I think that's technically a felony," Reyna says, letting go of Veer's elbow to snag her hoodie from the floor and offer it to her.

Veer shrugs. She's feeling very generous towards the world at large now. She's back in her body, she convinced someone not to become a murderer, and she's seen enough action movies to know that this is the point when the hero gets the girl. "Nah, we sorted it. Had a whole adventure in her head. It's chill."

"You walked through someone's mind and it's *chill?*" Reyna says, starting to smile now that it's confirmed she won't have to fill out any forms.

"I promised you a trick," Veer says, with her best imitation of a Hollywood leading man's smile. "My magic needs some skin-on-skin contact, though. Maybe we can go back to your place, and you can let me show you just how chill it can be?"

Like a lightbulb going out, Reyna's face shuts down to a look of disdain that is, quite frankly, a little hot. "I have a girlfriend," she says. She spins on her heel and starts to exit the room.

"No worries. I'm not a homewrecker," Veer calls after her, getting over her disappointment. And, she figures, if she's going to burn her bridges, she might as well burn them thoroughly. "She can come too!"

Reyna pokes her head back in, flips her off, says, "You're a piece of shit," and leaves for good.

"Hinge it is," Veer says, shrugging. Then she remembers Roop is still here. "In a women-respecting, God-honouring way, of course. I'm going to change *all* my habits since you spared me."

"*Leh*," Roop says, packing all the doubt she can into that halting, rasping syllable. "You'll stay young. Stupid, foolish."

"And ugly, and a disappointment to my parents," Veer jokes. Roop ignores her. Her face is still blank, but there is despair in every line of her.

"I stay here," Roop says. "Lie down and wait to die."

Veer almost says, "And you'll deserve it." But Roop thought she deserved it too. Deserving is bullshit, she decides, and she takes a deep breath. *Nirbhau, nirvair.* Without hate, without fear. She reaches out and gently helps Roop settle into a sitting position. She takes the spare hair tie off her wrist, gathers Roop's thinning grey hair, and starts to plait it into a simple braid.

"What are you doing?" Roop says, her voice expressionless from surprise or the Parkinson's. Veer's heart jackhammers: part of her is convinced that any second Roop will change her mind and steal her out of her body again. She still doesn't know why Roop spared her. But nothing happens.

"You look like shit right now, so I figured I'd help you not look like shit," Veer says, keeping her voice casual, tying off the braid. Roop has a lot of breakage—the braid won't last half an hour just tied at the bottom. Veer takes out her own braid and uses the elastic to reinforce Roop's at the base of her skull. "Where's your jewellery?"

"Why?" Roop says, but Veer picks up the answer through their proximity and pulls the case out of her nightstand. She recognizes some of the gold inside as the same set she had on in her kitchen, so Veer grabs out the heavy *jhumkas* to fasten into her sagging earlobes.

"When we go to the club next week, I don't want to be embarrassed when I'm seen with you," Veer invents. She slides the gold-and-enamel bangles onto Aunty Roop's wrists. "You're going to have to wingman since you ruined my chances with Reyna today. Do you still wear your wedding ring?"

"My fingers swell. It hurts me," Aunty Roop says, raising shaking hands to stare at her own wrists. The bangles clink against each other as she does. Veer decides against putting in her nose ring — someone else's boogers on her fingers, gross — and gets up, but Aunty Roop grabs onto her forearm. "Why are you doing this? I'm not your teacher or your *dadi.*"

"Course not," Veer says, ambling over to the exit when Aunty Roop lets go. It's times like these she's thankful she can read minds. Aunty Roop's face says she wouldn't piss on Veer if she was on fire, but when Veer heard her thoughts, everything was brightening and unfurling like yellow roses in spring. "My *dadi* refuses to talk to me until I find a husband. On the other hand, she's not a body-stealing psycho, so I think I'll stick with her instead of trying for a replacement."

"Manveer?"

"Yeah, Aunty?" Veer says, turning back. Aunty Roop opens her mouth, then closes it. Veer wonders if she's going to tell her never to come back, or if she's going to ask Veer to stay. A few minutes ago, Veer had been ready to die. What had convinced Aunty Roop to spare her?

Aunty Roop looks at her lap. Her earrings clink with the movement. "Turn the TV to *Indian Idol* before you leave."

THE MYTH OF THE FAMILIAR

EC Dorgan

EC Dorgan *writes weird fiction and horror stories on Treaty 6 territory near Edmonton, Canada. Her short fiction appears in anthologies such as* Northern Nights *(Undertow Publications) and* Afterlives: The Year's Best Death Fiction *(Psychopomp), and in magazines such as* Gamut, Hexagon, *and* Reckoning. *She is currently working on her first novel. We first published her in Issue 41 with 'Mooneater', and 'Flehmen Grimace' and 'Watercolours' were runners-up in the 2023 Raven Short Story contest, appearing in Issue 43. We're delighted to have her back with a softer touch of horror*

©2025, EC Dorgan

The Myth of the Familiar

The myth-maker wears fuzzy socks and works at a table. She's very old. She hasn't spoken in a long time. Her familiar is a Maine Coon called Mac. The cat sleeps in the bread basket while the myth-maker works.

You'd think a myth-maker would use a fountain pen, but this one uses dough. She bakes with the oil from her fingers. Sometimes a hair falls into her batter. She forms the stories into shapes—pretzels for tragedies, little round dough puffs for heroic sagas.

Though heroes are hard to come by these days. Something's gone off with the recipe. The myth-maker can't figure it out; she's been using the same flour for eternity.

One day, the myth-maker's AC unit fails. The kitchen gets hot. A drop of sweat from the myth-maker's temple falls into the batter.

The myth-maker pauses. She knows the five-second rule, but this is something different. Should she throw it out or start over? The myth-maker considers. She's not on a fixed schedule but she prides herself on efficiency. Her production numbers haven't faltered for three thousand years.

She looks at the batter. Except for the sweat, it's perfect. The myth-maker thinks about it. She's not one of these bakers who livestreams their creations. There's nobody around to see.

The myth-maker harrumphs. It's decided, no one needs to know. She resumes her work on the batter. But now while she's kneading, she feels eyes. She looks up and sees the familiar. The cat stares, and at that moment, the myth-maker knows — if there's one thing she's learned birthing stories all these millennia, it's that cats see everything.

The myth-maker shakes her head. Cat or no cat, she'll continue baking. She works the dough into shapes. She preheats the oven. She drops her dough puffs onto the hand-oiled tray: one, two, three, four.

When her timer goes, the myth-maker opens the oven and holds her hand for a moment in the heat. She grew up with a wood-stove and though she's now using convection, she remembers how to gauge heat with her hand.

Today the heat's perfect, like the little round puffs she's formed with her dough. She puts on oven mitts and pulls out the tray. The little puffs are perfectly browned, and she doesn't need a toothpick to know they're cooked through. The dough has risen just right.

The myth-maker sets the dough puffs onto the cooling rack and turns off the oven. As per her custom, she steps outside to nap in a hammock tied between two elm trees. Her familiar watches from the bread basket. Its whiskers are vibrating and its tail flickers.

The myth-maker sways on her hammock in the breeze. Her eyes are heavy. She likes the soft sun and the gentle shade of the trees. The touch of the early fall breeze. Golden leaves are starting to fall on her, but she doesn't mind—they'll add golden notes to her stories.

She lets sleep take her. She's expecting the same old plot lines. But today she dreams something altogether different. The myth-maker's been dreaming since time began. Today's dream is the first one since the dinosaurs that's something else entirely. It takes the myth-maker's breath and, for a moment, her spirit leaves her in her hammock. It soars into the trees and stretches to the stars.

She starts to stir but resists waking. She fights to stay in her sleep, even though the allotted thirty minutes have passed. If she lingers, her bread puffs will harden.

She forces herself awake. When she opens her eyes, she remembers every minute of that incredible dream. But she can't for the life of her envisage it. It was too much for her eyes.

She walks into her kitchen and stops. Sniffs, looks around. She's been making myths long enough she knows when something is off. She scans the counters. She can't put her finger on it.

She plucks her dough puffs from the cooling tray. Her familiar watches from the bread basket as she pops them into her mouth. One, two, three … She stops chewing. Where is the fourth puff?

Mac stands and stretches in the bread basket. His eyes meet hers. The myth-maker remembers that indescribable dream. Her eyes widen.

The cat walks across the counter with its tail up. The myth-maker stops breathing. The cat's belly is already hanging.

By the time the myth-maker is pregnant, the cat is already huffing and making strange sounds through its teeth. When the myth-maker's water breaks, the cat has already delivered a myth.

The myth-maker births three swashbuckling sagas. She opens her kitchen door to let them out, and they shudder through the earth like shockwaves, jolting the subconscious of every person on the continent.

But it's the cat-myth that's the strongest. All these years watching her work, that cat never touched that dough. Not till today, when it got the piece with the hero-making sweat.

The myth-maker shakes her head when she realizes. All that time, that's what was missing from her recipe. She'd gotten too good at working her dough. She'd stopped sweating. And heroes weren't born.

Overnight, all the dogs from London to Lisbon start barking. The internet's flooded with memes of all the hounds of the world collectively baying. Mice scream in darkness, and influencers post videos of panicked shrews.

A hero stalks the subconscious of every person, mouse, and cat. They call it the prowler of dreams. Now at night, people dream of hisses and strange cat battles. Eerie moans in dark alleys and crooked skies with strange stars. The only places to hide are cardboard boxes and paper bags. Some people find high perches.

The myth-maker can only watch from her hammock in her fuzzy socks. She's not used to being a familiar. But what choice does she have? Mac kneads batter with oiled paws. The cats are baking new myths.

PLAYDATE

Patrick Barb

Patrick Barb is an author of weird, dark, and spooky tales. He is currently living (and trying not to freeze to death) in Saint Paul, Minnesota. His published works include the dark fiction collections The Children's Horror *and* Pre-Approved for Haunting, *the novellas* Gargantuana's Ghost, Turn, *and* JK-LOL, *as well as the novelette* Helicopter Parenting in the Age of Drone Warfare. *He is the editor and publisher of the anthology* And One Day We Will Die: Strange Stories Inspired by the Music of Neutral Milk Hotel.

©2025, Patrick Barb

$\mathcal{P}$LAYDATE

The new boy ran inside the house, a kindergartener-sized blur of wild hair and limbs round with baby fat, moving too fast for Celeste to see who it was as he beelined down the hallway to her son Joshua's room. It was as if the phantom child had visited before — and had the layout of Celeste and Joshua's home committed to memory.

In contrast, the new boy's mother took her time, walking down the cement path, ascending the porch steps one after the other, gripping the black iron railing.

Her fingers were too long, too skinny.

Her smile reached Celeste before she'd made it to the door. "Well, hello there, Mommy," she said, applying the same cheery intonation as the postnatal nurses after Celeste's labour with Joshua had ended.

This new mother grinned, stretching hot pink lips that barely contained too many teeth. One of her eyes seemed bigger than the other. *Too big.* Almost bulging from its socket. But when Celeste blinked, those strange features receded as if they were never there.

The new boy's mother was fine. Normal.

She looked like any other mother. She almost looked like Celeste.

Determined not to seem flustered in front of a stranger, Celeste introduced herself with a practised business-lunch smile.

The new boy's mother shook her hand then crossed the threshold into the house. She kept her grip tight, pushing Celeste back as she stepped forward. Not forceful enough to offend. Just enough so it was as if Celeste had pulled the woman inside her home.

"My little one's told me so much about you," the new boy's mother said. She reached back and pulled the front door closed behind her, cutting them off from the world outside.

Just a silly figment of my imagination, Celeste thought. She kept her smile in place. *This is what mothers do, right? We keep smiling when someone's looking, even when it doesn't make any sense.*

Mothers smile through the pain, the confusion, and those too-quiet moments when the sharp edges of words might make their insides bleed.

"Oh, he has?" she asked her uninvited guest, the woman she hadn't known would be there, let alone inviting herself inside. Celeste left out the follow-up that she wanted to add.

"And who is he?"

With a wink, like the women were old friends trading barbs about ex-spouses over bottomless brunch mimosas, the new boy's mother leaned in close and whispered, "You can call me Dusty's Mom."

Dusty's Mom's breath smelled of honeysuckle and fresh-cut grass.

Two years before, Joshua had moved into a big-boy bed and cried through the first few nights, finally passing out in the early morning. Celeste had sat in the rocking chair beside his bed for hours, telling him about visiting her Pa-Paw's farm when she was a girl. One night, she whispered about the time when that exact combination of fragrances (honeysuckle and cut grass) became her favourite.

"My happiest memory," she told him.

"Until me?" he'd asked, eyelids finally weighed down with impending sleep. "Until I was born?"

"Yes," she said, "of course. Until you were born."

Joshua slept that whole night through, reassured of his mother's love and devotion.

But I'm not even sure I was telling him the truth, Celeste thought.

Celeste considered how the woman, who had a boy like hers and smelled like her childhood, referred to herself as 'Dusty's Mom' and nothing else besides.

She shuffled backward, moving deeper into the house, stealing glances behind to ensure she didn't collide with an end table or trip over some stray toy truck abandoned in the hall.

"Whose mom?" she asked, even though she'd heard the other woman perfectly fine the first time.

"Dusty. Your Joshua is all my Dusty talks about at home. Joshua this, Joshua that, Joshua's my best friend. I'm sure it's the same thing here."

Celeste nodded. Slow, uncertain. Her throat suddenly dry, her hands tingling.

They reached Joshua's room and found his door closed. Through wood painted robin's-egg blue, Celeste heard her son dictating the terms of play and pretend for the new boy who'd run through their house so, so fast. "And then Dinosaur Man came and then he came and he saw the bad guys and — hold this one, Dusty, okay? Then Dinosaur Man said *rawwwr* and he went …"

She couldn't hear if her son's companion replied. She didn't hear anything from the other boy at all. If she hadn't seen him rush past, Celeste might assume *her* little boy was all alone, talking to himself behind the blue door.

She reached for the silver doorknob. Before she could grab it, Dusty's Mom wrapped her too-long fingers around her host's wrist. "No, no, no," she said. "Let's leave our boys alone to play."

For a moment, Dusty's Mom had no face. No eyes, no ears, no nose, no lips, no teeth, and no tongue. Instead, her face was a swirling grey mass of squiggly lines, the same as the faded storm-cloud pattern Joshua had scribbled on the wall of the dining room a few months earlier.

He'd told Celeste he didn't do it when she found him sitting on the floor near the wall, pressing peanut-butter-and-jelly-sandwich-sticky hands against the pencil marks scratched in deep enough to cut through paint layers.

"If you didn't do it, then who did?" she'd asked.

"Dusty," Joshua answered, all matter-of-fact, the way kids do sometimes when they can't comprehend how their parent could be so stupid.

Except she knew the names of all the kids on the block and she checked the rosters of both preschool classes at Shining Promise Montessori. There wasn't a boy or girl named Dusty that her son could've known. Certainly not one who would be at their house.

If Dusty was a friend, he was an imaginary one.

But the woman standing beside Celeste, stopping her from opening the door and seeing her son, had come there with a boy named Dusty.

Celeste considered that maybe she didn't want to know where this Dusty had come from. Maybe she wanted to run, to hide under her covers until she was all alone.

Not all alone, but . . .

"Uh-oh, Spaghetti-O's!" Dusty's Mom sang in a pre-K cadence. Black eyes ran down her face like raindrops streaking across a windowpane.

Then, in a deep baritone, like a child putting on a grown-up voice, she said, "Let's go drink coffee and gin. Grown-up drinks."

Celeste steeled herself against this maddening absurdity, putting her foot down and taking a stand for a version of reality that made more sense.

"No."

She wrenched her hand free from Dusty's Mom. The woman who shouldn't have existed left red marks pressed into Celeste's pale skin. Free at last, Celeste reached for the knob on Joshua's door, twisted, and pushed it open.

Inside the room, Joshua looked up at his mommy with blue eyes glistening.

Come on, baby. Your friend and his mommy have to go. They have to go right now. Come on, come to Mommy.

Too late, Celeste realized that her desperate, imploring words sounded only in her mind. Too late, she saw her son smiling, looking first at his mother and then at a spot behind her where Dusty's Mom waved.

"See, Mommy! Dusty *is* real. You were wrong about him, Mommy. Right, Mommy?"

Right, Mommy?

Standing in her kitchen, pressing the white porcelain of a coffee mug into her palms, Celeste's breaths came in fear-filled bursts. She couldn't recall how she'd made it to the kitchen. A child's voice echoed down the hallway.

Is that Joshua?

"You told your boy that my boy, my Dusty, wasn't real. But he came from my tummy. My Dusty's daddy loved me, so we made a baby and he grew up to become a big boy. How could you say mean, mean things about my Dusty?"

"Excuse me?" Celeste defaulted to the tone she used when playground moms asked why Joshua didn't always take turns on the slide or when school parents pressed her about her lacklustre parents' support group attendance.

"I never said anything about that … that boy." When she tried to picture 'Dusty', Celeste saw a blur, a vibrating form next to her own son's face, going faster and faster until even Joshua's visage was erased.

"Nuh-uh," Dusty's Mom retorted. Celeste remembered Joshua speaking that same way, his still-developing brain trying to make sense of Celeste's rambling answer to his questions about where he'd come from. With insistent queries, he demanded to know more and more details about how Celeste and her dick of an ex-husband had brought him into the world.

"What are you?" she asked the woman — the mother — who shouldn't be.

Dusty's Mom smiled like she held a secret in her mouth, behind her thin lips.

"I am a Mommy. Like you."

"Where's your husband?"

"Where's yours?"

Celeste took a slow sip of coffee. It was perfect, just the way she liked it. "He's away," she said, "on business."

It was the same lie she'd told Joshua and that Joshua had probably spread to his friends, teachers, and anyone who would listen.

Another smile from Dusty's Mom.

"My Dusty's daddy does business, too. The boys have so much in common. That's how they became bestest friends. So much the same they could be brothers. Might be nice for yours … to have a brother, I mean. Might be nice to have a mother, too."

He has a mother. He has …

Celeste should have wanted to call for her son. She should have wanted him close, the way all mothers want their babies near at hand, especially when they're young and still getting a feel for the complicated and dangerous real world surrounding them.

But her boy's name got lost in her head. When she tried to bring it up, it eluded her.

Appointments and emails and business conversations, all the serious things she kept track of day after day, blocked the name from reaching her lips.

And why not? After all, those were things she *needed* to remember, information vital to keeping a roof over their heads, to keeping her boy fed, to keeping him safe.

His name was …

His name is …

"Dusty and Joshua play together every day. When you're watching, when you're not."

There it was. One of those names belonged to Celeste. She'd given it to the boy who'd grown in her womb—from a collection of cells representing a random selection of genetic material to a blood-slicked alien creature learning to breathe the polluted air of a slowly dying world.

All Celeste had to do was remember which name belonged to her. Then she'd know which boy was hers.

"The boys told me what you said to your son. 'Your friend isn't real. Stop lying. You liar, you little, little liar!' How could you say such things about my sweet, sweet boy to your sweet, sweet boy?"

The words sounded familiar enough, conjuring darker memories.

Hendrick's gin fumes wafted off each syllable, reminding Celeste of late nights when she would leave the child's bedroom before he'd fallen asleep. She left him crying because she ran out of words to calm him, to let him know she was there for him. All she wanted was to be gone.

At a certain point, she stopped wanting him to know she was there. At a certain point, a tiny part of her — maybe a not-so-tiny part of her — wanted him to believe she'd gone away forever. Just like his daddy had.

"My boy wants to be a race car driver dinosaur when he grows up," the woman with mismatched eyes and too-long fingers said. As though growing up to be a race car driver dinosaur was no different than heading off to Harvard or Yale.

"What does your son want to be?" the strange woman asked.

"I ... I don't ..."

Celeste pulled on the strands of hair wrapped around her fingers like she could snatch the correct answer free, bringing a wavy curl along with it.

"It's okay, Mommy," the mother said. She called her *Mommy* in a way Celeste was certain she'd heard before, but she couldn't remember when or what the context could've possibly been.

A boy ran past her kitchen. Celeste leaned forward, trying to peer around her visitor. She wanted to make sure she knew the face of the child. If she could see him, then she would know him. She was certain of it.

But she didn't get the chance.

He was already gone.

The visiting mother smiled at her. She placed her hand over Celeste's. Her touch was soft at first contact, then gritty as it lingered, like digging your toes past a top layer of smooth white sand at the beach to reach the scratchy bits of rock and shell compacted underneath.

She remembered her own Mommy — her mother — bringing her broken seashells, telling her they belonged to a mermaid. Telling Celeste that she was brought to her from a dream of a crashing wave, all bundled in seaweed and smiling, saltwater tears falling from her eyes.

"That's silly, Mama," she'd said. "That's not real at all."

Mother's words were almost swallowed by the roar of exasperated waves. "But can't we just pretend it's true?"

Celeste closed the door to her home office downstairs. She heard voices out front and wanted to make sure it wasn't the package she was expecting. Standing in the foyer, she pulled back one of the curtains from the bay window.

No mailman or delivery truck driver, though. Only a mother walking with her two small boys. Celeste couldn't gauge well, but she was certain both were around the same age.

One of the boys looked back the way they'd come. His soft, kind eyes caught hold of the woman watching him from her window.

We look so much alike, she thought. *Like he could be mine.*

Their mother stopped and rested a hand on the boy's shoulder before pulling him toward her. "Come on, Joshua," she said. "Let's go. You and Dusty can play all you want at home."

Joshua.

It was the name Celeste would've chosen if she'd ever had children. When she'd met a blind date for cocktails a few years back, he'd asked her what she'd name their hypothetical child. She'd drunk too much gin and found herself in a confessional mood. She was ready to go home with him and make mistakes.

She couldn't recall why she hadn't.

It had to be okay, though.

After all, the guy turned out to be an asshole.

Celeste let the curtain fall back over the window. She laughed, chastising herself for letting her imagination run wild and thinking the boy could be hers.

"Imagine me, a mother," she said.

The pain in her heart came suddenly, a live-wire shock.

She hurt so bad, it had to be something real.

THE SUICIDE MISSION

KR Segriff

KR Segriff is a Toronto-based writer and filmmaker. Her work has appeared in Greensboro Review, PRISM international, The Malahat Review, and Best Canadian Poetry, among others. She won the Edinburgh Story Prize, the London Independent Story Prize, and the Pulp Literature Bumblebee Prize for Flash Fiction. Her first collection of short stories, Animals in Captivity, was published by Riddle Fence Debuts in 2024.

©2025, KR Segriff

The Suicide Mission

Chief Vranic's lipstick ascends her lip fissures like lava rising from scorched earth.

Lipstick seems contradictory to her values, Brian thinks.

"Ah, Brownlea," Vranic says, "looking, as ever, like Mr Mark Wahlberg's ugliest brother. Why not peel back your face and show all of Beograd the droid beneath?"

Brian stares past Vranic to the Danube River beyond.

"I despise you, Brownlea," Vranic says. "But you might be my only agent who can succeed."

"Is it contempt or a deep repugnance you feel?" Brian asks. "Šta?"

"The definition of *despise*. A contempt or deep —"

"Bog! You Ameri-bots. Thank God the Agency reassigned me to Srbija, where people have half a brain."

"Had you remained in America, your daughter might not have fallen for the Russians."

"Better in Putin's arms than an American cowboy's."

"I suspect your preference would be to eradicate *all* possibilities."

"Men are, in general, bullshit, Brownlea. My Alexsandra would be CIA Director now if she had chosen to remain."

"Alexsandra is only thirty-three, so regardless of gender, it seems unlikely—"

"Enough. Back to your orders."

"Fine. The Genex Building is thirty-six storeys and inundated with BIA since the Russian crisis. One agent cannot penetrate. I need a team."

"It's a solo job, Brownlea. A black op. The hostage is a top-level asset."

"Entry is technically possible, but should I succeed, they will react. Lock down the building. It's a suicide mission."

"No such thing for you," Vranic sneers. "I trained you at Peary. Skills-wise, you were the best recruit I'd ever seen."

"Success at the Farm is a poor predictor of—"

"Bullshit. Special Ops 4 at twenty-four? Weapons, tacticals, and three classified qualifications even I can't access? You're the biggest overachiever the Agency has ever seen. It's disgusting. They wouldn't give you such a long leash if you were a woman."

"Individual women are statistically more likely—"

"Save it, C-3PO. Pay attention. Facial rec means no possible clearance to the inside. The hostage is on the seventeenth floor. East side."

"Over thirty feet, undetected external entry is impossible. How—"

"Old-school, Brownlea. They wash the west side windows tomorrow. The perimeter's card clearance only. We made a Jack-in-the-box to your specs. There are external blind indentations on both sides of the building. You go up on the window washer's platform, give it the slip on seventeen, and send the Jack the rest of the way up."

"And walk unharnessed into a blind alley at two hundred feet?"

"Still a weakling for heights, are you?"

Brian recalls the parachute pack pressing against his shoulders in 2 0 1 5, and the siren of Vranic's voice above the jet engine's roar as they tried, for the third time, to push him past the cabin door:

"Fear is your enemy, Officer! Dive through it!"

"It's impossible!"

"Do it for your bloody country!"

Those were the days when Brian still believed in good and evil. Though he conceals the shift within him, Brian increasingly suspects there is nothing in life for which he would jump from a plane anymore.

"Not a weakling," Brian says, slipping back to the present, "just more adept at determining the odds. In the present situation, it is preferable to refuse and accept disciplinary action."

"I remember a time when you were unquestioningly loyal."

"I remember a time you told me to stay away from Alexsandra or you'd have me fired."

Vranic snorts and pulls a paper from her pocket. "Just like that, Brownlea? Well, subtlety was never your forte."

Vranic slips the paper into Brian's open palm.

"It will almost be a pleasure to watch you fail."

Vranic turns back toward the city as Brian uncurls the paper. *THE HOSTAGE IS ALEXSANDRA.*

As the washer platform rattles upward, Brian considers the Jack-in-the-box mannequin lying beside him. From behind, it could be his twin.

How remarkable to look at oneself from an angle usually seen only by others.

The fourth floor slides past.

Irrelevant, Brian. Op mode. You're a machine.

Sixth.

Alexsandra is already dead. She killed herself the moment she went over to the Russians.

Seventh.

This is a mission to recoup Vranic's daughter. To you, she is nothing.

Ninth.

Brian readies the Jack for ascent and checks the winch. He realizes the mannequin's face is featureless.

If BIA surveillance notes the reflection, the cover will fail.

Tenth.

Incorrect. If they can see that close, we are already lost.

Brian pulls his backpack's strap and notes the reassuring weight of the equipment inside. Fibre optics, semi-automatic MP5s, and high-precision tools have replaced the Windex and shammies.

Twelfth.

Brian looks down, and that millisecond of weakness is almost his undoing. Sweat beads on his upper lip, and he closes his eyes. He will have to employ a mental distraction. He reviews the floor plan of his apartment in Novi Sad.

The empty hallways, the empty bed.

Thirteenth.

The empty picture frames. The empty evenings. The empty promises of America.

Fourteenth.

Brian. You are a machine. Focus.

Fifteenth.

Brian drops, presses his cheek to the plywood, and releases the winch. The Jack jerks upward into place. The blind end in the building's surface comes into view.

If you fall, it will be 6.39 seconds until impact.

Brian dangles his legs over the edge of the platform.

Sixteenth.

For Alexsandra.

Brian lands like a songbird on the thickened window ledge. The Jack continues upward on the washer platform without him.

For Alexsandra?

He presses his palms against the building's exterior and wills his feet to shuffle sideways toward the next window.

Irrelevant, Brian. Machine. Machine. Machine.

Brian extracts the laser cutter from the outer pocket of his backpack. Three clockwise circles, three shallow hits, and he's inside. The 'Three-Pane Entry Record' is 98.6 seconds, and Brian holds it.

Overachievement is not always a bad thing.

The office Brian enters is vacant, a fortunate side effect of the pandemic. Brian eases the fibre-optic snake-scope beneath the door to the hallway.

Two men guarding the stairwells, two at the entrance to the east corner unit; must be at least four on the inside. Fifteen seconds, on average, before the interiors notice and lock down the cage.

Brian bursts from the stairwell and lands in position.

Aim at the middle of the mass. One. Two. Three. Four. Scan the pass from the third body. And we're in.

Brian enters the corner unit and locates Alexsandra on a table in the room's southeast corner. She is bound entirely, save her head, in plastic wrap.

Taking no chances with her. Smart. At least some of their choices were optimal. Marks incoming. Shoot the closest first. The rest as they come. Avoid the southeast corner. Four. Three. Two. One. Done.

Brian steps past the bodies and secures the door from the inside. They will have some time before the others discover he's penetrated the cage.

He crosses to Alexsandra and rips the grey tape from her mouth.

"Looks like it's just us, Brian," she says.

"Clearly. You would have told me immediately if there were more."

"You trust me so blindly? After all our disappointments?"

"Yes."

"Why?"

"I don't know."

Alexsandra sneers her mother's sneer and indicates her wrapped body with her eyes. Brian extracts a box cutter from his pack and slices downward, his hand oddly unsteady.

"What's happened to you, Robot-Love? You used to be so precise."

She shakes loose the wrapping and rises unsteadily to stand beside him.

"We should only pursue this conversation," Brian says, "if we agree with my assessment that the chance of escaping alive is zero."

"It's not zero. Glass lasers?"

"Correct. Heir and the spare."

"You cut there." Alexsandra motions to the window in front of them. "I'll take the window in the side office. It exits above the blind ledge on the east side."

"Redundant," Brian says, taking the first cutter from his backpack. "You are better off covering for potential fire while I cut our single exit."

Alexsandra's smirk returns, and the penny drops in Brian's mind.

"Decoy exit," he says, embarrassed to have missed the obvious. He removes the second cutter from the backpack and throws it to Alexsandra.

Brian cuts his hole, meets Alexsandra in the east office, and finds her exit already prepared.

"Getting a bit rusty, my lovelorn drone," she says, and slides through the window hole onto the outside ledge.

"Lovelorn?" Brian says, hesitating at the exit.

"Yes," Alexsandra calls from outside. "The definition is—"

"Unhappy because of unrequited love. But that adjective doesn't apply."

Brian wills his feet forward to the outside ledge. Alexsandra looks back over her shoulder and says, in the gentle voice she used to reserve for their more intimate moments, "Steady, B-Ri." She slides her hand back inside the window and finds his.

Brian remembers the fourth jet run in 2015, the time he managed to jump. Alexsandra volunteered for the flight, and as Vranic hollered beside them, Alexsandra pressed her lips to Brian's ear and said, "Imagine it's already over. That we are flying together."

Brian steps onto the ledge. The world wobbles but quickly rights itself.

"There are several things unclear to me," Brian says, "and the most immediate is this: there seems no possible way down."

Alexsandra shimmies across the ledge and brings herself deeper into the blind end between the building's sections. Brian follows.

"Remember the street below us," she says. "When you scoped it, what was unusual?"

"Two Fiat Palios, same year and model, and an eighteen-wheeler between them."

"Exactly. When we go over the ledge, aim for the truck. On my go, she will inflate the rescue basket."

"She?"

"Mother, of course."

"Vranic? But how …"

Alexsandra presses her chin to her shoulder and says, "We are in the cave."

A faint voice speaks from somewhere near Alexsandra's right ear: "They are exiting front now. Is C-3PO with you?"

"Mother," Alexsandra says. "I didn't gnaw through the window with my fucking teeth."

"So the little *mašina* came for you?" says Vranic's crackly voice.

"We both knew he would."

"Bah. He will betray you eventually. He serves no purpose now. Why not push him over the ledge?"

"Mother, we have an agreement. It's a highly inopportune time for a pissing match."

"Highly inopportune? Listen to yourself. Always a little robot, just like him."

"Are they following yet?"

"Da, Alex. Wait for my go."

The sound of gunfire erupts from the front of the building.

"Ours are in the building across," Alex yells, "picking them off as they exit the decoy hole."

"Clearly," Brian says, "But how —"

"Input device implanted behind my clavicle, output behind my mandible. Stealth channel. Mother installed it when we decided I'd try Moscow."

"Who are you working for now?"

"Depends who you ask."

"Double agent?"

"Still America's fanboy, Brian? Our observations had indicated you might finally be over that adolescent fantasy."

"I have always wondered what would have happened if I had followed you to Russia."

"Ancient history, Brian. I don't know why I even asked you. It was clear to everyone, at that point at least, that your 'America, fuck yeah' vibes were too deeply ingrained for you to make any other choice."

"That assessment is valid."

"Have you not realized, in this world, it's every man for himself?"

"Correct," Brian says. "The goals have become disordered. The chain of command illogical."

Things always seem clearer when I can discuss them with Alexsandra.

"Exactly, Brian. And the data points are ever-moving, so we must follow them wherever they lead us. Every government will disappoint eventually. Mercenary is the only way."

She has always understood my mind.

"But we waited too long," Alexsandra continues. "The BIA is in bed with Russia. They took me because Putin knew Mother was faltering and wanted to force her hand."

"Faltering?"

"Losing her allegiance to Uncle Sam, like we all are. But they didn't realize that we're not looking for another government to lead us."

"We?"

"Those who have accepted the limits of human integrity and insist on exerting our autonomy over whom—or what—we serve."

Alexsandra turns to Brian, and he recognizes her expression, the distinctive flush of her cheeks.

She is nervous.

"Care to join us, Brian?" she asks. "Or would you rather join your faceless friend in the penthouse?"

Brian looks up to where the smooth-featured Jack lolls on his platform. Alexsandra's gaze follows.

"Mother is more complex than you know. She agreed to take you, but only if you demonstrated you could serve something other than a façade."

"So this was an elaborate test? She is maniacal."

"No. The opportunity simply presented itself, as we knew it would. Did you think it was a coincidence they transferred you to Belgrade?"

Alexsandra turns again to her right shoulder.

"Two incoming," says Vranic's voice. "Your exit."

Brian pulls his gun from his leg pocket, shoots two men as they exit the window hole, and turns his attention back to Alexsandra.

"Getting back to lovelorn," he says.

"Goddamn, Brian. You're as bad as Mother. Not now."

"I am following the data points, and where they fall factors heavily into my next decision."

Alexsandra sighs.

"Brian, are you happy?"

"No."

"Are you in love?"

"I don't know."

"Yet you scaled a building with no clear exit, against all reasonable calculations, simply because you discovered I was inside."

"Correct."

"And would you say the reason you cannot be happy, despite your obvious personal successes, is that you are without love?"

"I don't know."

"Brian, drop the automaton mask just for a second. The only time you ever say 'I don't know' is when you are afraid to face a truth."

She always expresses herself so clearly. This is why I feel more comfortable with her than those who are less logical.

Alexsandra's earpiece buzzes.

"Go time," Vranic says.

Brian edges across the ledge to the front of the building, and Alexsandra follows. Brian looks down.

"There is only the truck below us, Alexsandra. This is suicide."

"The basket takes 4.7 seconds to inflate. There is time. Trust her."

"Your mother hates all men. And your relationship with her has been inconsistent. How can you be sure?"

"Not all men. Mostly just my father, who chose Mother Russia over her."

"And she has projected this betrayal onto 50.4 percent of the population?"

"Don't you see, Brian? Against her natural inclinations, she has chosen love again."

"For me?"

"God, Brian. Stop sucking the tit of your Y chromosome. She chose me. My own chance at happiness."

Alexsandra's earpiece buzzes again.

"What did she say?" Brian asks.

"Loosely translated: Get your pathetic asses down here before I change my mind."

The world wobbles anew, and Brian starts to tremble.

"Your accusation of 'lovelorn' is possibly incorrect," he says.

"Jesus, Brian."

"Alexsandra, is my love unrequited?"

Alexsandra's mouth curls up into a sneer but expands to a smile.

"Brian," she says, taking his hand, "we are already flying."

As they step from the ledge and plunge toward all that expands beneath them, two words cross Brian's mind.

For love.

THE ORANGERY

Mark Gallacher

Mark Gallacher *is a Scottish writer who lives in Denmark. He has been twice shortlisted for the Fish Short Story Prize and was runner-up for the 2021 Wigtown Poetry Prize. His sci-fi novel* Saved From the Fire *was released by Ringwood Publishing in 2021.*

©2025, Mark Gallacher

$\mathcal{T}$HE ORANGERY

You have one brother and five sisters. William. Marianne. Olivia. Silvia. Melissa. Angeline. The brother you sometimes forget but not the sisters. The oldest sister, Marianne, passed away a week ago, optimistic as ever, slipping into a final contented coma. What did she die of?

She died of congestive heart failure.

It's the kind of gently corrective thought generated by some of your mods that is supposed to mitigate failing memory. Dates. Names. Relationships. Facts. A breeze of data cascading in the background to keep dementia and infirmity of thought at bay. And to hide your tendency to forget awkward facts. But increasingly, the mods make you feel like you are a tourist inside your own mind. Who put all the data in there?

You did.

You crossed two continents to get to Marianne's bedside and silently told her to shut up, because whatever she was telling you, with that hint of a smile on her dead face, you knew she was right.

At your great age, strong feelings rarely bloom. You have an airy, wintry mind. So when the sudden wave of intense grief swept through you as you stood by Marianne's deathbed, you looked away and smiled a strange, quivering smile. Like your heart was wreckage sucked up from the silt of time.

Silvia, never one to avoid a scene, asked what was so amusing.

You muttered something unintelligible — an old man's defence — and reached for the silk handkerchief in your shirt pocket, the one Marianne had given you forty years before. But you'd lost it thirty years ago in Singapore, hurrying out of an art museum, looking for a taxi. You can't remember a thing about the art museum, but you can remember the taxi driver's face.

The Hope Singapore International Museum of Arts. Founded 1960. You visited the Hian Retrospective Exhibition on 16 May 2072.

"I just learned my ex-wife is dead," you had wanted to tell the taxi driver. All the art in the world rendered stupid and meaningless. Instead, you rasped, "Airport." You spent the rest of the journey wondering how you could still have been in love with her and not known it, and what that meant for your second wife — which turned out not to be very much, because she was already making secret arrangements to divorce you. Something else you didn't see coming.

"You don't even know how to cry properly," Silvia said, but the other sisters admonished her with tuts and disapproving glances.

The humanist funeral was this morning. 'Clair de Lune' and some Tartan-soft music piped in over the speakers. It made you think of a whisky commercial you saw on an airplane years ago. The brand you can't remember.

Old Ailsa Craig Single Malt.

When Marianne's coffin was driven away, you could have drunk a whole tumbler of the stuff, just to feel something burn inside.

Now it's mid-afternoon and the sisters move around the great garden, naming plants and trees. Marianne's lifelong work to create harmony. One of them asks, "Who will look after the orangery now?"

They all murmur in the negative. They glance back at you. "Not me either," you say.

Angeline reaches out. "Come on, James! We're going back inside." And you feel like a lost boy, hurrying into their midst. Melissa, the youngest sister, takes care of practicalities, feeding people who insist they aren't hungry. Silvia carries cups and plates away. Melissa's and Silvia's children and grandchildren stand around the periphery, trying to find protocol and rules for the first death among the family's late-centenarians.

Dying is not as frequent as it used to be. And that's down to you and your bio-inventions people call mods. You can't stop people from becoming ill or dying from doing stupid things, but the ones who avoid calamity last longer. Thanks to you, some of the people gathered here will live to 160, some even to 180. More second acts. More second chances. More time to try and forget old regrets. This has made you wealthy beyond imagination. You watch your sisters work the rooms. Embracing children. Patient with everyone. It's a gift you don't have. Your awkwardness is made worse by your failing memory—one of the downsides of living so long.

But despite the forgetting, old memories resurface like freshly stunned Lazaruses, stepping out of the tomb of oblivion in vivid Technicolor. Beautiful, terrible memories. People long dead, as clear and sharp as springtime. Ghosts reaching through time.

Ahead of you is the bathroom.

The mods have sensed that you are becoming aimless and that you should urinate soon. You blink and take stock. Your childhood home is an airy gothic artefact. Despite Marianne's many renovations and modernizations, she could never remove its secret paternal darkness. All the homes you have lived in since have been modest, minimalist designs, full of light and air. You cannot stand nooks and crannies, shadows and stairs. Rooms with keys.

You need to use the bathroom. You are slightly dehydrated.

"Shut up," you say out loud, and the mods go quiet.

You wander through the rooms. Who are you looking for? People nod or avert their gaze. Where's William? You remember and feel foolish. The youngest sibling has found a pub down the road. Family gatherings were never his thing. He is probably amazed that he has outlasted any of you considering he refused most of your mods out of some kind of spite.

At last you find a soft chair to sit down on. All this walking and remembering is exhausting.

A small boy runs up to you. Extends his hand. "I'm Leonard," he says, like it's an achievement.

"Which one is your mum?"

Leonard points to a mousy-haired young woman in a black dress.

"Hmm. Which one is your grandmother?"

Leonard shakes his head. "She couldn't come."

"Well, then, which one is your great-grandmother?"

Leonard points to Melissa, who is fussing with some large vases of pale lilies and white roses.

"She's strict, I bet."

Leonard nods but it isn't clear he understands *strict*. "She says you're an egomaniac."

"Egomaniac?"

"Yes."

"Well, maybe sixty years ago. Do you know what that means?"

But Leonard has lost interest. He runs away.

You catch Melissa's attention, and she comes over.

"He's a feisty one," you say.

Melissa rubs her arm. "Not like his father."

"Which one is he?"

"Oh, for god's sake! Do you have dementia?"

"Very likely. My synapses are losing fidelity. I am in decline. I lessen. I wither."

"Don't be such an old thespian. You don't have the talent for it. Jeffery's over there. Is this going to be your party trick for the rest of the funeral? Pretending you can't remember anyone? With all that AI trickery inside you?"

You focus on Melissa's hands. She rubs her arms like there's worry in the bones. You remember those arms, swollen and bruised after your father threw her to the floor like a rag doll. How old was she then? Eight? Nine? His rage was monstrous, like darkness you could not contain.

"Some things I can't forget. By the way, the flower arrangements are lovely."

Melissa stops rubbing her arms. Studies your face. Leans down and gives you a soft kiss on the cheek. "Thank you," she says.

"Where are the others?"

"In the orangery. Where else? Come on. Take my arm. Let's go see them."

You make your way into the hall, Melissa by your side. Leonard is with some other children, sliding down the banister at speed. You remember playing the same game lifetimes ago. The memory is full of ache and fear. Your father roared somewhere in the huge house and you all scattered to hide.

You find the other sisters inside the orangery, sat on an oak bench that still has your ancient shaky initials carved under a coat of varnish.

"Come and have a glass of wine," Angeline says, raising her glass like she's forty-five and could last the whole day drinking. Olivia shifts along the bench. You sit down heavily. Angeline pours you a glass.

"I don't think my mods will allow it."

Angeline smiles. That tight, ironic smile that she has. You haven't seen her laugh in seventy years. She offers you the glass and you take it.

You remember her kissing a girl in this orangery. How old was she then? Seventeen? Her red hair ablaze in a beam of sunlight. The heady citric scent of oranges and lemons everywhere. What was the name of the girl? Your mods are silent. You could do it the old-fashioned way and ask. But you're afraid Angeline has forgotten.

"I read you were donating your huge fortune to saving the polar bear," Angeline says.

"Not true," you tell them. "The polar bear is doomed, I'm afraid. Less than a hundred left. You know, you can always call me and ask—or visit me."

"Much too busy to be visiting trillionaires," Angeline says.

"Me too," Olivia agrees.

"I have created two foundations," you tell them. "The Mars Colony Foundation and The Longevity Research Foundation."

"Still dreaming of immortality," Angeline quips. "Don't we live long enough?"

"I stopped chasing that illusion thirty years ago. I just hope for another decade of relatively good health."

"I'll drink to that," Olivia says and raises her glass to her lips. You note the slight tremble in her hand.

"I can fix that," you say.

"Oh, leave it be," Olivia says. "Must everything be fixed? It's only nerves from the stress of today."

You are happy to sit silently for a few minutes, your sisters on either side. It is a pleasure that you want to savour now that you have lost Marianne.

"Then there were six," Olivia says.

Angeline sighs. "Who'll be next to slip this mortal coil?"

"You look fit and healthy," you say. "All of you."

Your sisters murmur approvingly.

"Who gets the house?"

Your father's last twist of the knife. Leave everything to Marianne and hope the siblings would fight over it and hate each other. But they never did. Marianne kept the house and lived cheerily alone. Happy with her garden and music and home building projects.

"I don't know," Olivia says.

"You don't know? I thought you helped her write her will."

"She changed it a couple of times without my help. So I don't know."

"I suppose she cut me out because I was so rich?"

"For god's sake," Angeline interrupts. "Does it matter? None of us need money."

"What about William?"

"Money would kill him."

"So nothing for William either," you say.

"Honestly, James," Angeline snaps. "It's ridiculous. You don't need anything."

"For the record, I'm not the richest man on the planet. Not by a long way. I would like to have the books. That's all."

Angeline raises an eyebrow. "Daddy's old books? You'll never read them all."

"For my library. Which I'm donating to the university when I die."

Angeline tuts. "You should have asked Marianne when she was alive. People can't read your mind."

"Thank goodness for that. Well?"

"I'll talk to the lawyers. I'm sure no one cares about the books."

Silvia takes a deep breath and straightens her skirt and fusses nervously with her blouse, a sure sign she is about to say something. "Well, I'm glad we're all here and we have a moment's privacy. Marianne wrote you something." She takes a letter out of her skirt pocket and unfolds it.

Well, sibs, my time is up and I'm checking out and there's nothing we can do about it. James's mods can't stop it coming. I just wanted to tell you that I love you all and that you have all turned out remarkably well despite Father having been such a monster. I know you're hearing this in the orangery because we always end up in the orangery. Though I'm sure William has found the local watering hole down the road. Tell him I love him. Tell him not to be so hard on himself. Most of all, tell him there's still time to turn things around.

I have one special request. Do not bury me next to Father. Put me next to Mother. In case you forget, I've put it in my will. So I guess it's not a request at all. It's an order.

I wish I could have stayed a little bit longer and, yes, I have a few regrets, but fewer than I supposed I would have. Keep my grave tidy. Don't forget me. I'd like to linger in the collective memory for a while. Please share any stories you have about me. Good or bad. Funny or sad. Pictures. Film clips. I don't care.

Don't be strangers, and try to be kind to each other. Goodbye.

P.S. Yes, James. You can have the books. Apart from 'Delirious' by Sophia Ringwater. That's for Angeline.

How did she know? Marianne, the clever one.

On the way back to the house, you ask Silvia if you can borrow the letter. She is reluctant to give it to you, but you promise to give it back.

Later, you can't resist going to the study. You browse through the shelves. You find the book and open it. Inside the cover is an ancient card with a red rose printed on one side. On the other side, written in neat letters: *For Angeline. First love of my life. Susanne.*

Whatever scent it held has long gone, the ink faded to ghostly shadow.

But your mind is suddenly bright with remembering. Susanne was the girl Angeline kissed so hungrily in the orangery. The shock of their passion made you dizzy.

They hadn't seen you there. What were you doing? Hiding from your father on one of his drunken rages. You had tried to sneak away but saw your father coming down the path.

"Father's coming!" you shouted, stepping out from your hiding place.

Then Marianne came running from the house and ran past him, blocking the door to the orangery. Ready to scratch his eyes out if it came to it.

And Angeline seized Susanne and kissed her again.

Your father stopped, as if slapped in the face. He wheeled around and staggered away, with rage to burn. He found William and beat him so badly he limped for days. Olivia hid somewhere in the house, waiting until all the shouting was over and the damage was done.

Susanne. A dark-eyed girl who had been all mysterious watchfulness. You met her decades later. One of those bio-AI conventions you used to go to. There was music and wine. Too much wine. Flirting turned into something else. A hotel room with a view of tall, glassy skyscrapers. Susanne telling you, if only you'd been older back then, she would have kissed you instead. How differently things might have turned out.

The next morning you said your goodbyes in the foyer, booked on different planes, headed for different continents.

You put the book back for Angeline to find. For her own ghosts to come haunting.

You find the pub where William is holed up.

He is the youngest but looks the oldest by a long way. Proof you can still let yourself go to ruin. You can lead a life of perpetual self-harm.

William bristles at the sight of you when you enter. You see the shadow of your father. But it is only a shadow.

You take out the letter. You suspect he is too drunk to understand. You read it to him anyway. You try. For Marianne. For your mother. For yourself.

William lets out a long sigh and gives up his anger. He wipes his eyes.

"You want a drink?"

Alcohol is not advisable with your current state and medication.

You tell the mods to shut up.

"Sure. I'd love a drink."

It seems the most natural thing in the world. To sit there. To sip the drink. Soon, you think, he will tell you a story about Marianne. One you don't know.

DARTH VADER VS TESTICULAR CANCER

Mike Carson

'Darth Vader vs Testicular Cancer' was chosen by Diana Gabaldon and Donald Maass as second runner-up in the 2024 Jack Whyte Storyteller Award at the Surrey International Writers' Conference. This is the eighth SiWC placing for **Mike Carson**, and you will be able to see his winning story, 'M4R1NR', in our upcoming Autumn issue. You can find his previous runners-up, 'Andouille' and 'Deep Water,' in Issue 38, Spring 2023, and Issue 26, Spring 2020, respectively. Mike lives in Kamloops, BC with his wife, his sons, and a small surly dog.

©2025, Mike Carson

$\mathcal{D}$ARTH VADER VS TESTICULAR CANCER

Harry Bonner knelt beside the neatly made bed. "Dear Lord," he said, "please give me the strength to guide these young people away from the darkness and into the light." He raised his head, looking past his shelf of Star Wars collectibles, to meet the sad-eyed gaze of Jesus staring at him from the crucifix above. "Or at least stop them from using their idle hands to vandalize the school with obscene graffiti." He stood and straightened his tie in the mirror. There were some other issues too, but the Heavenly Father, he was sure, had seen his suffering. If the Lord wept at the fall of a sparrow, what must He have done when he'd witnessed Harry trying to scrub a crudely drawn penis off the wall in the boys' bathroom? Yes, there had been some rough patches in his first weeks as vice-principal, but, having engaged the devil in battle, Harry was not about to back away from the fight.

"Amen," he said.

Downstairs, Harry kissed his wife on the back of her neck as she stood at the counter. Meg turned towards him. "Honey," she said, brushing a piece of lint from Harry's collar, "don't let the bastards grind you down."

Six blocks away, Harry paused, briefcase in hand, just outside the gates of Lord Melbourne Secondary School. It was still early, and the campus was calm. He looked back wistfully across the street at FM Rogers Elementary, where he had taught Grade 6 for nine years. Though he hadn't appreciated it at the time, they had been the best years of his life. What happened over the summer after elementary school, he wondered, that turned happy kids into angst-ridden monsters? Perhaps it was high school itself, collecting and assimilating children like some massive Borg ship and turning them into passionless, cell phone–addicted cyborgs. Harry shook his head. He had to keep things in perspective. Of the nearly 1,700 students who attended Melbourne, most were reasonable albeit unenthusiastic students. In the two months he had been there, Harry found ninety percent of his time was spent dealing with the same small group of incorrigibles.

Then there was Dylan Bain. In that recidivist ten percent of miscreants, Dylan was a category of his own. The boy spent more time in the office than the principal did. Frequently, as Dylan sat in detention spitting bits of paper at the supervisor or watching inappropriate videos on his phone, Harry had wanted to check the boy's scalp for the mark of the beast. It was in those times of tribulation that Harry prayed for patience. After all, was it not for the sake of young people like Dylan that God had sent him here?

He climbed the grey concrete steps, past the bronze statue of the school mascot, the Melbourne Mule, and entered the sunlit main foyer. Inside, someone had stuck a sign to one of the front windows. *Hi, Welcome to Hell,* it read. Gladys, the senior office assistant, threw a half-hearted wave in Harry's direction as he headed down the hall to his windowless office.

Ten minutes later, like a storm cloud borne on a current of Chanel No. 5, Principal O'Connor blew into Harry's office, her angular face set in a cold frown. She closed the door behind her. Babs O'Connor had always reminded Harry of a stick insect: she was long-limbed and thin, had a penchant for olive-drab outfits, and spent most of her day trying to blend into her surroundings.

"I just got off the phone with Misty Meadows, Lucifer's parent," Babs said. "She was very upset."

"Lucifer's mother's name is Misty Meadows?" Harry said, shaking his head.

"It's not a joke," Babs said. "The students can't learn if they feel marginalized. Ms Meadows fully supports her child's autonomy. We need to do better—and Pendergast needs to get off his high horse and start treating his students with more respect."

"And you think calling a Grade 8 student 'Lucifer' is appropriate?"

"I'll admit it's unusual," Babs said, "but Misty Meadows has a huge online following. She has her own parenting channel on YouTube. This story is already blowing up all over social media—#namenazis has gone viral."

Harry didn't see her point. He was fairly certain that calling someone a nazi was considerably worse than *not* calling someone Lucifer, but he kept quiet as Babs continued, "If we don't want this to become a massive shitshow—with the superintendent, the board, and the mainstream media all over it—we need to get ahead of this. It's not the hill we want to die on."

"What hill do we want to die on?" Harry said.

Babs smiled, little cracks forming just below her cheeks. "I know this is all new to you," she said, "so just listen to me. Go talk to Mr Pendergast, get him to apologize to Kayleigh-slash-Lucifer.

Apologize to her yourself. Keep apologizing to people until this blows over."

"Even if I believe it's wrong?"

Babs walked to the door, opened it, then turned to face Harry again. "What you believe is irrelevant," she said. "The only thing that matters is who has the loudest voice, the most followers—they're the ones who get to say what's right or wrong."

Harry shook his head. "You're the boss."

"Now you're learning," Babs said as she walked away.

Harry did as he was told. As a reward for abandoning his principles, Kayleigh/Lucifer called him a fascist again. Mr Pendergast called him a "Bible-humping wimp," threatened to go on stress leave, and concluded by saying that Harry would be hearing from the teachers' union.

Harry rounded out the day literally sniffing out vapers and pot smokers, chasing down skippers and vandals, and breaking up fist fights and TikTok feuds. "So this is 'educational leadership'," he said to himself as he slumped down at his desk at the end of the day. Maybe he wouldn't die on this hill, but he was certainly taking a beating on the way up.

Harry spent a few moments in silent prayer, then gathered his things for the upcoming staff meeting. He was looking forward to this one. Some of the 4-H kids had asked Harry to present a fundraising opportunity to the staff. Harry was especially proud of the fact that Dylan Bain was a member of the club—the boy had even made some slides for him to use. It was a triumph, just the sort of wholesome activity Harry felt certain would put Dylan, and kids like him, on the right path.

The 4-H Club's plan was to use the school store to sell nutritious, homegrown produce to staff and students. Harry's only regret was that he hadn't had a chance to look over their presentation beforehand. *Oh, well*, he thought. *It will be more authentic this way.* Most of the staff had already arrived by the time Harry got to the library for the meeting: everyone tried to get there early so they wouldn't have to sit near the front. Babs got things rolling by spending thirty minutes going over a list of administrivia that could definitely have gone out in an email. The staff sat slack-jawed, staring at their phones, grading papers, and letting out the occasional sigh. Only Mr Pendergast was looking up, glaring at Harry.

"Finally," Babs said, "a reminder to keep students away from the north field. The broken sewer main has been repaired, but the ground is still very soft. The area has been roped off until it dries." She exited the slide deck on her laptop and turned to Harry. "Okay," she said, "I got 'em warmed up for you."

"Great," Harry said, addressing the staff. It felt like talking to an oil painting. "I respect your time, so I'll get right to it. The students in the 4-H Club have asked me to share an exciting fundraising activity with you, a presentation they have worked extremely hard on. Even Dylan Bain—I believe many of you know Dylan—took part."

Ms Doerksen, one of the English teachers, popped her head up from behind a stack of papers. "Dylan Bain," she said, "is the devil."

"No," said Mr Pendergast, still skewering Harry with his unblinking stare, "Lucifer is in my class."

"Maybe that's the problem," Harry said. "We've given up on these kids without really trying; we've written them off when maybe, instead of our scorn, they need our support. A little direction, a little compassion. I think the least we can do is listen." He opened the file and cast the 4-H Club presentation onto the big screen behind him. "Their idea is to sell wholesome produce from the school store."

He advanced to the first slide. *Cornhub!* it announced in bright, bold letters. *Come wrap your lips around one of our big, buttery cobs.* Behind the text was an image of a large corn cob aimed at an open mouth, dripping with what looked like butter. A lot of butter.

It took ten minutes to restore order. After that, the meeting was over — there was no coming back after Cornhub was launched — and the teachers filed out, wiping their eyes and chuckling. "Best staff meeting ever," one of the shop teachers said.

Later, in the now-empty library, Babs explained to Harry about the infamous pornographic website with a name a lot like 'Cornhub'.

"But how would teachers even know about something like that," Harry said, "let alone the kids?"

"Harry," Babs said, patting his arm, "you are a good person. Maybe too good." As she walked away, she said over her shoulder, "Have you considered that high school just might not be the best place for you?"

Harry sat in the darkened library until he was sure everyone had gone home. Later, as he trudged down the deserted hallway towards the distant exit, he noticed that every bulletin board now had a Cornhub poster on it. Whoever had made them had taken Harry's picture from the school website and Photoshopped a jester's cap on his head and a massive corn cob in his mouth. *Meet Cornhub's New Mascot,* announced the banner at the top, and beneath it was the caption, *The Cob-Gobbler*. As he pulled down the posters, Harry felt his heart hardening against Dylan Bain and the 4-H Club students.

A sadder, wiser Harry awoke the next morning. He lay there, staring at the ceiling and considering calling in sick. Then he remembered that it was Halloween and, despite his disapproval of the festival's pagan roots, Harry never missed the chance to dress up. With renewed energy, he sprang from bed. At FM Rogers, his Star Wars–themed costumes had always been a hit with the children, and this year's Darth Vader get-up promised to be his best yet. Besides, the chance to hide his face behind Vader's mask for the day appealed to him somehow.

Later, as he was fastening his cape, Meg came and sat on the bed behind him. "Harry," she said gently, "do you really think the costume is a good idea?"

"What do you mean?"

"It's just, well, the kids at Melbourne seem a lot more, uh, worldly than the ones at your old school."

"Everyone loves *Star Wars*."

"I don't," Meg said.

With a swish of black polyester, Harry whirled around and stared at his wife. Stung by betrayal, he said simply, "I have to go." Then, gathering up his lightsaber and tattered dignity, he stomped out of the room.

Taking a page from Babs's administrative playbook, Harry had planned on spending the day cloistered in his office, but an uproar in the hallway just after the first bell forced him to investigate. In high school, the sound of children's laughter is rarely a good thing.

As Harry emerged into the main foyer, he was surprised to see a large, erect, inflatable penis bouncing down the hallway. Arms protruded from each side of the purplish shaft, aggressively swinging a hair-stubbled burlap scrotum like a scythe, leaving a swath of giggling Grade 8s sprawling in its wake. Harry stepped into the path of the oncoming penis, blocking the ball with his arm as it swung towards him.

"Hey, Mr B," the penis said. "Nice costume. Did you come to tell me you're my father?"

A smirking face protruded from a hole in the shaft, right about where the frænulum should be. It was Dylan Bain. "Dylan," Harry said, as calmly as he could while a throng of students gathered around, holding up their phones, ready to be entertained, "go home. Now. Change into something appropriate for school, and then come to my office. We have a lot to discuss."

"I'm a dick," Dylan said. "Everyone here's seen a dick before. Bet you've even got one under that plastic banana hammock, right, Darth?" The gathered students shouted agreement. "Besides, it's for a good cause: I'm raising awareness about ball cancer."

"*Testicular* cancer is not a joke," Harry said, "and your costume is not funny. Change it immediately." The crowd clearly disagreed. "Okay, Boomer," someone shouted.

"My grandpa only has one nut," Dylan said, picking up his scrotum and slapping the single ball inside, "but I think maybe he was in an accident or something."

"What's your point?"

"Gramps loved my costume. Thought it was hilarious."

"I'm only going to ask one more time," Harry said, "and

then I'm going to recommend that you be expelled from this school." He turned to the crowd. "And the rest of you get to class immediately, or you'll find yourselves in detention."

The students began shuffling away. A few clutched their throats, pretending to choke. "Careful, he's using Jedi mind-control on us," one said.

"What class do you have first?" Harry said, turning back to the offending penis. "I'll let your teacher know you'll be absent."

"English," Dylan said. "Dorky Doerksen won't care, though."

"I'll let Ms Doerksen know," Harry said. "When you come back, we'll talk." He watched as Dylan turned towards the main exit, dragging his scrotal sack behind him.

Harry was feeling pretty good. That whole situation could have gone sideways quite quickly. He shoved the Darth Vader helmet down on his head. *Why not give the kids in Ms Doerksen's class a chuckle?* he thought.

"Hello, Mr Bonner," Ms Doerksen said when she opened the door. "Are you here to promote Cornhub?"

"How did you know it was me?" Harry said.

"It could not have been anyone else," she said, shaking her head.

"Dylan Bain won't be in class today," Harry said. "His costume was highly inappropriate."

"Good."

"I'll keep you posted."

"Don't bother."

Ms Doerksen turned back to her class, "Sit down right now!" she said to a group of students gathered by the window. She walked over, glanced outside, then turned back to Harry. "Was Dylan dressed as a penis?"

"How did you …?"

"Well, either Dylan didn't go home, or there's another large penis running amok in the girls' outdoor ed class."

Harry rushed to the window in time to see a group of Grade 11 girls laughing and dodging the rampaging erection as it charged their ranks. Like young matadors, the girls whirled away at the last second as the penis trundled by, its enormous ballbag bouncing along behind it.

The world went red inside Darth's helmet. Roaring and brandishing his lightsaber, Harry charged from the room, down the long corridor, and out onto the field, his cape streaming behind him. "Dylan Bain!" he shouted as he neared the frolicking phallus. "Stop right there."

When Dylan spotted the enraged Sith Lord running towards him, he turned and fled, but his progress was seriously hampered by his costume. Holding his lone ball before him, Dylan speed-shuffled towards the north field. When he reached the roped-off section, he dropped and rolled under the barrier, with Harry right behind him.

But running in the Vader suit was no joke, and Harry was flagging. Breathless and sweating, nearly blinded by rage and condensed perspiration inside the sweltering helmet, Harry failed to see the rope Dylan had avoided. He hit the barrier at a full run and flew head first into the spongy ground of the north field, his lightsaber bending beneath him. He struggled to his feet just in time to see Dylan trying to clear the far fence. He was almost over when the costume's oversized ballsack snagged on the chain link. The penis hung there, slowly deflating, arms yanking desperately at its entangled scrotum in a vain effort to free itself.

Harry struggled to his feet. He tried to run, but the ground was too soft. He could feel it sucking at his boots, dragging him down. As he collapsed into the stinking ooze, he became aware that a large crowd had gathered. The entire school was outside, holding up their phones, pointing, jeering. Over the din, he heard Lucifer laughing.

With howls of derision ringing in his ears, Harry rose, picked up his mangled lightsaber, and slunk towards home. He couldn't show his face at school again today, if ever. He went upstairs, took off his mud-befouled costume, and tried to pray. But when he looked up at the crucifix, even Christ's compassion seemed to have turned to contempt. Harry's heart felt dry as dust.

When Meg got home from work, she put her arms around Harry. "How was your day?" she said. Then she started to laugh.

"Not you, too, Meg," Harry said. "I'm humiliated."

"You're an idiot," she said, hugging him, "but you're a famous idiot."

"What are you talking about?"

"Hashtag-darthvdick is trending. It already has 700,000 views on Misty Meadows's Instagram." She held up her phone for Harry to see. "My personal favourite is the GIF of Darth Vader sword-fighting with a giant penis, though."

"I can't go back there," Harry said.

"When you're going through Hell," Meg said, "keep going. They can only beat you if you quit." Meg turned and started walking up the stairs. "Besides, some good came of it," she said. "Apparently that Dylan Bain kid told everyone his costume was supposed to raise awareness about men's health issues. The Testicular Cancer Foundation's website crashed because so many people were trying to make donations. It was on the news."

"It's on the news, too?" Harry said.

She turned back towards Harry, smiling. "Come on," she said, holding out her hand. "Sitting around all day looking at dick pics has gotten me a little hot and bothered. Why don't you come upstairs and show me your light sword, Mr Vader?"

"It's a sabre."

"I'll be the judge of that," Meg said.

The next day, Harry got to school two hours before anyone else. He was sitting in his office researching overseas teaching jobs when Dylan Bain came in.

"Hey, Mr B," he said. "We're famous. We should start planning our costumes for next Halloween."

"Dylan," Harry said, "please leave me alone."

Instead, Dylan sat down.

"You've ruined my life," Harry said.

"Nah. You're a legend now."

"For being a penis-obsessed madman," Harry said.

"Whatever," Dylan said.

"Shouldn't you be in detention?"

"I'm going. I just thought … well, I just wanted to tell you I know I've been a dick. Literally." Dylan stood. He looked smaller somehow. "I know you're mad," he said. "Just don't give up on me, okay?"

He stopped in the doorway and turned back towards Harry. "Oh, you should probably check out the boys' bathroom on the second floor," he said. "Whole lotta dicks spray-painted on the wall up there." He shrugged. "Kids, huh?" Then Dylan went out, closing the door behind him.

And Harry wept.

THE 2024 RAVEN SHORT STORY CONTEST

© 2 0 2 4, Shanley Kearney, Emily Groot

THE 2024 RAVEN SHORT STORY CONTEST

It was another exciting year for our flock of Ravens — both returning and new — as part of our annual short story contest. We wish to extend a full-hearted thank you to all who participated in this year's contest and to those who continue supporting Pulp Literature Press. We also thank our fantastic, endlessly talented judge, Kelly Robson, who was once again burdened with choosing just one winner out of so many exceptional stories. In her own words, *"Many of this year's stories eloquently conveyed the anxiety and instability of our current moment, exploring these existential fears through a wide variety of settings and points of view — historical, far future, extra-planetary, extra-human. It was an honour and a pleasure to read them all."* However, the journey must eventually come to an end, and we congratulate those at the front of the flock this year.

First Place: **'The Mall We Deserve' by Shanley Kearney**

Runner-Up: **'Providence' by Emily Groot**

Further congratulations are for those flying close behind, our shortlisted 2024 Raven authors and their stories:

Sophie Ganic with 'Frequency Eight'
Debbi Hofsink-Borst with 'The Train Inside'
Katie Lawrence with 'The Feeling'

Laura MacLeod with 'Silly Games'
Jennifer Moss with 'What Cassandra Saw in the Water'
Melody Sundholm with 'A Toast to the Rich, the Gullible, and
 the Damned'
Mitchell Toews with 'Parade Day'
KT Wagner with 'Old People Climbing Stairs in the Dark'

__Shanley Kearney__ received her BA in Creative Writing from the University of Southern California and lives in San Francisco, CA. Her fiction has been published and awarded in Phoebe Journal, Flash 500, and 3rd Wednesday. She has worked for four high-profile tech startups and co-founded her own in 2023, serving as its CEO. She can be found on her YouTube channel @shanleyjanekearney and on Twitter @shanleykearney. She is currently looking for a literary agent to represent her debut novel.

__Emily Groot__ is a public health physician, born and raised in Sault Ste Marie on the territory of the Garden River and Batchewana First Nations. She now lives with her family in Sudbury. 'Providence' was inspired by the true story of the 1849 cholera outbreak in Bruce Mines.

The Mall We Deserve

by Shanley Kearney

There was a mall in Springfield that would take you back to the eighties. Blue and orange lights lined the walls of coin-fed arcade games. The indoor fountain was year-round and its water circulated upwards and sideways while shoppers sat and stared, losing time. A food court made up the entire west wing of the second floor and sold fried pickles, pizza by the slice, blue raspberry smoothies that turned tongues bright purple, Coca-Cola fizzling in thick Styrofoam, gyros made by the Costas family, and subs, of course. The hallways were wide and crowded with red-and-blue patterned carpet and grey tiles. Escalators to the second level were popular to slide down on. At the entrances were hot pink signs: *Stay Long.*

The people of Springfield referred to it only as "Our Mall."

Our Mall had every store both needed and wanted. But there was always space for more down the line. Victoria's Secret, Hot Topic, GameStop, T-Mobile, Coach, Bath & Body Works, Foot Locker, Ulta, Nike, Teavana, Macy's, Zales, RadioShack,

Bergner's. There were lines in these stores at the holidays, on weekends, and even on school nights in Springfield.

There was a time before Our Mall—when it was Eastland Mall. It was a lifeless waystation of a place—pass through, grab what you need, continue on. Then people started to linger and then they started to stay. At some point, Eastland Mall was sold to a different management company. Not many remember it.

"Jamie, I'm going to Our Mall. Would you want to meet me there?" Amy Arnolds asked over the phone, clutching the perfect yellow landline she bought at RadioShack the other day. Which day, she probably couldn't recall.

"Oh, yes! I need a few things," Jamie Marks said, thumbing through her purse.

They went, along with their strollers and baby bottles. Their older kids ran ahead, making their way to the arcade and food court. Benjamin, Ally, Emily, and Daniel saw everyone from their school through the windows of stores. Lily Adderson, known among many as the teacher's pet and time-waster because she raised her hand and gave answers that started with *Thank you* and *That reminds me*, jumped into a cloud of perfume, sniffing the air before she even pressed the nozzle. Jackson Moore tossed into the air a baseball that he'd picked off a shelf. The ball soared high, higher than he thought it would, almost grazing the lights attached to the ceiling. "Sorry," he yelled as an employee came running over. Mrs Roberts, the seventh-grade English teacher, stopped to talk to a pair of parents pointing proudly at her star student. She left quickly, spotting the parents of her least favourite student, whom she just gifted a failing grade to.

"What do you need first, Jamie?" Amy asked. Her head was on a swivel, noticing everyone she knew.

"I need to head to Macy's for some kitchen towels," Jamie said.

"Oh, perfect. Maybe let's stop to talk to Margaret first. I just saw her in Kohl's."

"Yes! It's so funny," Jamie laughed to herself, "I see more people I know here than when I go to church."

The air in Our Mall smelled like salt. It was briny like the Pacific Ocean, which is saying something for the landlocked people of Springfield. In fact, there was salt everywhere. Salt in the fries, the oily pretzels, and the jumbo-sized bags of chips sold at the food court. There was sour salt in the quips from the teenagers working at Hollister: "No, we don't have *anything* in the back." There was sweet salt in the air near the kid's playpen, where kids ran amok, thundering down the slides and roughhousing their way through dismantlable foam blocks like the future linebackers some of them would be. Sweat glistened on their small temples and dripped down their noses. The parents sneezed. Salt of the earth, these folks.

Of course, too much salt made them thirsty.

So they went back to the food court, sat by the water fountain, and drank out of striped straws. They sat under a narrow skylight. It was like being outside, but better.

"I have to get going," Charlotte Porter said to her friend. "Adam will be done with work soon. Time to prep dinner and then get the kids to bed."

"Have Adam come here." Michelle smiled widely. She had unusually large teeth. "You can just eat in Our Mall. I can call Stephen, and he can meet us here, too."

"That's an amazing idea! How did I not think of that?"

Our Mall had consequences, subtle at first. Larger later.

They were all so healthy in the mall. Pink cheeks. Limber joints. Loud laughs and silky throats. Clear noses. Quick feet. Strong arms and shoulders. Less so outside.

"Hi, Jamie," Amy Arnolds said, pulling up to Jefferson Elementary School.

"Hi, Amy. I'll grab Benjamin and Ally from the gym." Jamie smiled tightly.

"I don't know how you do it — volunteering for pick-up. I'm so tired all the time." Amy laughed.

"Well, some of us know how to dig deep." Jamie turned around briskly.

The kids presented pamphlets to the parents given to them by the teachers, "Cold Going Around" printed boldly across the tops of the pink paper. The families rolled their eyes, smugly reteaching their little ones how to wash their hands. "Now, don't forget."

The cold came, and then stayed.

Half the town was sneezing. Half was coughing. This was bad but not dire. The doctors handed out prescriptions for antibiotics and called it a day.

They breathed easier at Our Mall. Surrounded by Christmas decorations — "Brendan, can you believe it's December already?" — they sipped on peppermint coffees, took photos with Santa, and tried on heavy coats to protect them from the cold. Outside was desolate, and there were thick sheets of snow and icy wind. They preferred to stay inside, in Our Mall.

The trees were sick, too, but it was hard to tell because it was winter and things died in the winter. Forgotten sticks on the ground, old leaves covered by snow, it was all the same. Though it wasn't.

A fog descended on the town gradually. One day, the clouds just seemed thicker. Like an innocent layer of cream cheese. But they also looked heavier.

"Justin, when was the last time you saw the sun?" Austin Reed asked, typing away at his computer. Insurance was the industry of this town.

"Not sure, boss."

Then the clouds lowered. Quickly, everything became coloured in murky greys with dingy air that resembled a sick person's saliva. The roads were slick. It was hard to drive to school, and the kids were sent back with new pamphlets in their backpacks: "Driving Advisory—The Fog."

But the roads to Our Mall were clearer. Tires had traction on the road there.

Julie Baker died first. She'd tailored the homecoming dress of every girl in town, working out of an eight-by-eight carpeted spare room in her house. She had four boys, each of whom played a different sport, and she sewed each team's uniform. The doctors couldn't figure out exactly why she died, but her lungs resembled those of a lifelong smoker. No one had ever seen her smoke.

Julie was a PTA mom who baked cookies for every bake sale and distributed flyers to join the parent prom committee. She made sure her boys had fresh lunches filled with protein and special cheeses. All this is to say she was very busy. And she had little time to visit Our Mall often.

Two weeks later, Marcus Brooks died in the middle of the night. He worked as the regional president over at BrightGuard Insurance. His wife handled the shopping. His lungs resembled Julie Baker's.

A week later, two local vagrants died outside a 7-Eleven while the sun rose, its garish winter light shining down on their lifeless bodies. Maybe at this point, suspicion would have started to rise, but they actually were smokers, among many other things, and they had no one to shout their names in outrage and ask, *"What is going on here?"*

It took six more deaths before paranoia settled into the town's psyche: Laura Elizabeth, a farmer's wife who hated social interaction; Eleanor Ruth, an old woman living with her daughter's family; George Harris, the owner of the town's Walmart; David Lawrence, one of the town's best and only lawyers; Sarah Langford, that lawyer's only secretary; and Richard Winslow, or Father Richard to his parish.

The fear settled into people's bones gradually — "Maybe let's take the kids to the mall after school? Just to be safe?" — and then irrevocably. Much like the fog.

Our Mall's sales only rose. No mall in America experienced the massive surge in sales Our Mall did, even accounting for the holidays. First, a state-wide newscast picked up on the story — "The Little Mall That Could" — but soon it crossed state lines, and by the end of December, it was a national story.

Forbes quickly assigned two junior writers to research and put together a formal case study on Our Mall and the town's booming economy. "Find out how other towns can replicate this, Jimmy." *The Wall Street Journal, Bloomberg,* and *Fortune* quickly sent their own representatives after hearing about the budding story. But it wasn't just business magazines, though they had a particular, hungrier interest — publications like *The New Yorker, The Atlantic,* and *The Chicago Tribune* all followed the scent of the story soaked in Americana and Midwest suburbia.

Only about half the writers and researchers made it home. Once back at their desks, they wrote little and talked even less. The others could be split into two groups: dead and alive. The ones who fell sick did so rapidly after arriving and then died just as quickly. So quickly that the families assumed their illnesses and ailments had predated their travel and arrival. This prolonged the issue for the town—it would have been helpful to have some loudmouthed outsiders poking around and asking, *"What is going on here?"*

As for those who lived, well, they liked the mall. Convenient hours—"Open Late"—the best cinnamon lattes they'd ever had, bright purple railings to lean over and see the tops of people's heads, every store they could think of, intellectually stimulating artwork decorating the walls, and a movie theatre that was set to open by the end of the week.

Stay Long.

Amy Arnolds threaded her hands through the cord of her yellow landline. "Jamie, do you ever think about what it was like before Our Mall?"

Jamie coughed profusely. "Sorry about that," she cleared her throat. "Not really. I mean, why do you ask?"

"I just …" Amy trailed off. "Sometimes I wish we could go back."

"Go back?"

"Yeah, to before we had it."

"Wait, you mean get rid of Our Mall?"

"I don't know," she sighed. "Never mind my nonsense. I'll meet you at Macy's at five?"

Jamie nodded and then remembered Amy couldn't see her. "Yes, see you then."

Other people started talking like this, too, but only with utmost caution. These were radical ideas. Worries were muttered in whispers and admissions came out stuttering. Dick Myers, the Catholic high school's football coach, was so scared to speak about it that he only uttered his first suspicion to Father Peter in a confession booth, his mouth inches from the latticed wood opening. Father Peter, still deep in his grief for Father Richard, nearly pushed aside the screen. "I've been thinking the same."

Some were quick to shut down such ideas. The Costas, owners of the gyro shop in the food court, were able to buy a second house in town and create trusts for their five children. The other food court families were in similarly victorious shape. They spent the most time in Our Mall, manning fryers and cleaning smoothie blenders, so they were confused when people mentioned "the sickness."

"What do you mean? People are sick?" Eleni Costa said to Stephanie Sullivan, who owned the neighbouring pizza shop with her husband.

"That's what people tell me." Stephanie shrugged. "But I haven't seen a single person cough here."

"Maybe it's in their head. People always think they're sick in the winter."

"They'll be fine once summer comes."

Summer came, but without the colour green. The trees, bushes, and grass had long since died, with no one to notice. This was barren land. No seed could grow.

July was a dead, faecal yellow. Grass broke in the slightest wind. Skin flaked and fell, while IV tubes ran dry.

Our Mall was drenched in colour, bleeding rainbows shamelessly: gluttonous hot pinks, emeralds, fuchsias, corals, bright turquoises, and radiant ambers.

Our Mall now offered apartment living.

They — what was left of the town — came in the night. They arrived with screwdrivers, sledgehammers, crowbars, mallets and chisels, power saws, jackhammers, a bulldozer and crane someone had rented from a construction company that asked few questions, the local garbage company's dump trucks, and a wrecking ball the city planning committee was able to anonymously provide.

Everyone wore face coverings — safety goggles, dust masks, hard hats — to protect themselves from flying debris, but these veils were helpful for other reasons. No one knew exactly who showed up that night to dismantle Our Mall. Was that Linda Jefferson, the elementary school's office assistant, hammering into a neon pink *Stay Long* sign, or was it Amy Brooks, one of the many pink-wearing PTA moms? Did John Bradford, a respected regional manager over at BrightGuard Insurance, drive the bulldozer that shattered the Macy's crimson storefront display, or was it Adam Porter, who worked on his team? There was no formal check-in or paper trail of communications identifying who brought what. Whether the assault was premeditated or spontaneous was never clear. It just was.

By sunrise, Our Mall was dead. The expansive plot of land lay hollow. There was little said about it. Not even the kids asked questions.

People stopped dying, but the cough lingered. A scratchy, hacking, convulsive cough. After people started to leave, the surrounding towns could recognize the former Springfieldians by that barking.

The people of Our Mall.

$\mathcal{P}$ROVIDENCE

BY EMILY GROOT

Henry Nicholls had hoped to be a poet, although he had no business with hope or poetry. He'd grown up in a two-room house in England and left school for the Cornwall mines at age ten. Now, on the north shore of Lake Huron, in a damp cabin a short walk from what would come to be known as Canada's first copper mine, the rain and late-season mosquitoes kept Henry awake. The air was thick, too humid for Henry's sweat to dry, sticking his sheet to his back. He shuffled in his bunk, trying to find a cool spot.

There was no clock, but Henry felt the sleepless hours passing—a frustration he had known since arriving in Upper Canada from Cornwall. Despite the clouds, the cabin was brightening. Sleep would not come now. It was Sunday, and the rain would make for good fishing after church. He stretched and left the cabin for the outhouse while the seven other men slept.

My dear Sarah,

I have received news of a cholera outbreak in Sault Ste Marie, possibly extending to Bruce Mines. I am leaving immediately, although I fear my medicine will be useless. I apologize I was unable to say goodbye in person. I expect to return in a fortnight. I am unsure how this disease spreads. I will quarantine myself from you after my return.

With love,
Wilfred

Henry was right: the fishing was excellent. The clouds had given way to weak sun and sticky air. Henry and another miner, Anselm, used the herring that crowded by the shore as bait for larger fish. They cooked one lake trout for lunch and smoked two others. Although the bushes had been picked over, there were enough blueberries to each enjoy a handful. Anselm offered his handkerchief when the purple juice streaked down Henry's chin.

Anselm was the most beautiful man Henry had ever had the pleasure of seeing. Anselm had bright blue eyes not yet dulled by work underground. They had met, these two Cornish men, by impossibly small chance in the busy port of Montréal. They shared the trip to Bruce Mines together, and Henry fell in love as soon as Anselm's rough hands had brushed against him. Now, they shared a semblance of a life together in these woods. They could never have a house in the village, no, but they could share meals and work and sleep, and wasn't that almost the same?

Flies found the fish guts they had thrown into the forest, their buzzing interrupting the silence that follows rain. Henry joked that it could almost be music.

"Better flies than mosquitoes," answered Anselm, slapping the back of his neck. He turned his hand to show a streak of blood.

Henry wrinkled his nose. "This godforsaken place," he said. "Just the bugs are enough to drive me mad."

"Money's not bad," said Anselm, wiping his palm on his pants. He lowered his voice to add, "Company neither."

Dear Sarah,

I will probably have returned to you by the time you receive this by post. Apparently a woman and her child died in Bruce Mines after returning from Sault Ste Marie. They have already been buried, I am told. I have also heard that the Ojibwe moved west across to Lake Superior to avoid whatever is fouling their land around the St Marys River.

Yours,
Wilfred

At the bottom of the shaft ladder, Anselm fixed a candle to Henry's hard hat with clay. A small kindness explained by love, but one that might simply be ascribed by any observer to efficiency. Anselm's freckles disappeared in the candle's dancing light, but the kindness in his eyes remained. Henry clasped Anselm's hand for a short moment, hidden by the flickering shadow.

Swing, scrape, shovel. Swing, scrape, shovel. There was a rhythm to the work in the dark, excavating ore and sending it to the surface in buckets. The air tasted of black powder and seeping water. But the biscuits and fish wrapped in cloth in their pockets still kept their proper taste even when eaten underground. Anselm and Henry sat next to each other to eat. It was cool in the dark, but they both smelled of sweat. Lunch took only a few minutes, and then they returned to freeing copper from the earth.

A ringing bell let the miners know their shift was finished. A short line of men climbed the ladder back into the sunshine, blinking, not knowing cholera was stalking them.

"Do you want to take the long way back?" Henry asked Anselm. "I want to stretch my legs."

Anselm paused long enough to appear as if he did not already know his answer. "Yes, all right," he said in a considered tone.

Another miner waved goodbye as they left the main path. The trail was narrow and required them to walk single file. Occasionally one of them would slap at a mosquito. The birch leaves fluttered in the breeze, showing alternating shades of green.

Believing them to be far enough from the mine, Henry stopped. Before he could turn around, Anselm's arms wrapped around him from behind. Henry felt lips on the back of his neck and wished he could have washed off the dust that he was sure coated his skin.

A twig snapped. They hurriedly stepped apart. Someone was rounding the corner, approaching on the path that went down to the docks. Henry could make out Dr Wilfred Ulster striding towards them. The doctor's pace did not change, and his face remained impassive. Had he seen them?

"Hello, Doctor," said Henry.

"Hello, boys," the doctor said in his usual clipped tone. "Are you both feeling well?"

Henry and Anselm nodded.

"And the other men? Any reports of illness?"

"No, sir. Nothing I've heard of," said Henry. Anselm shook his head in agreement. They both moved off the path to allow the doctor to pass. Dr Ulster moved quickly, carrying only a small black bag.

In return for a small monthly fee, every man in the mining camp received care from Dr Ulster, usually for sprains and broken bones. The doctor was physically a small man, born near Kingston, who had studied medicine in Montréal and interned in New York. His service in the Battle of Lundy's Lane was permanently etched on his face, and he was never seen to smile. He visited the camp at the start of every month, the journey on steamer a great expense to his own time and not entirely covered by the camp payment. Distracted by what Dr Ulster may have seen, Henry and Anselm did not consider that this was his second visit this month.

Once the doctor was no longer visible through the birch and pine, Anselm laid his hand on Henry's shoulder.

"I am sorry."

"Love covers a multitude of sins," said Henry, smiling weakly.

They walked back to the cabin, remaining a measured distance apart.

September 2, 1849 — I examined Colin Agar and Samuel Smith in their tent. They are men in their thirties. Both lay curled on the ground. Both had diarrhoea and cramping; Colin also reported vomiting. Their skin was as dry as paper. Both men professed extreme thirst, but I was unable to convince either man to drink much. They gagged and heaved even with small sips of water.

A certain quiet terror seized the camp. A person could go to sleep well enough, lose control of their bowels overnight, and be found dead in the morning. Children in the village tried to rouse their parents only to find them too weak to leave their beds. Neither the miners in the camp nor the village could guess who would get sick and who would stay well. A husband who dug a grave for his wife not once felt a twinge in his belly, but a boy in an otherwise well family, too young to leave his house alone, died after a short course of diarrhoea.

Henry was convinced that a combination of fresh air, fasting, and prayer would protect him. Having spent two lonely and boring years in a sanatorium as a child, Anselm was less sure. But because it lessened the fear in Henry's eyes, Anselm bowed his head with Henry every night before bed, although he did not go so far as to give up any meals.

"O God! To us, may grace be given. Father, Son, and Holy Spirit, here I am. We are not our own. We are yours. I yield to you, but please spare us death. Amen."

Anselm closed his eyes while Henry prayed. They sat side by side on Henry's bunk, space between them but close enough to feel the warmth from the other's body.

"I am scared," Anselm said when Henry was finished, "to die so far from home."

Henry looked around the empty cabin and then took Anselm's hand. "We work in the dark every day. And still God finds us underground."

Anselm traced the calluses on Henry's palm.

"I am not afraid," Henry said, his kind voice threaded with a fear that undermined his words.

September 3, 1849 — The camp privy is insufficient for the frequency of use. I note that ill men are emptying their bowels in the bush, or in their beds if they are too weak to stand. On examination, their stools are thin and watery. They keep their sunken eyes shut.

Henry sat down heavily on the ground, flexing his feet to loosen his cramping calves.

"Are you all right?" Anselm asked.

Henry leaned his head against a birch tree. His tongue felt too large in his mouth to answer. He closed his eyes and shook his head. The movement made him dizzy and hot. Despite his fast, Henry could still feel the contents of his stomach clawing towards his mouth. He vomited onto the soft forest floor.

Anselm offered him his handkerchief, still stained with blueberries. Henry wiped his mouth and closed his eyes.

"Just let me rest for a few minutes. And then we can walk back."

Henry left the trail three times to empty his bowels on the short walk back to the cabin. He gripped Anselm's forearms when his cramping legs exploded in pain, crying from the torment and exhaustion of it all. Anselm tried to wipe away Henry's tears, but found only dry cheeks.

Leaving Henry in his bed, Anselm left the cabin and returned with Dr Ulster.

Henry opened his eyes without moving his head when they entered. "I don't understand. I have been praying." Henry spoke to himself as much as to Dr Ulster.

"This sickness is not a matter of providence," the doctor said curtly. Dr Ulster inspected Henry's face, pulling down Henry's lower lids and looking closely at his lips. He pinched the skin on Henry's abdomen, which stayed peaked like a little tent even after Dr Ulster removed his fingers.

The doctor turned to Anselm. "Give him as much water as he will drink, maybe some broth. Nature is cruel, and cholera is not under God's sovereignty."

September 3, 1849 — Henry Nicholls, age 19, a miner, reported he had been suffering from leg cramps and diarrhoea for two days. He was lodged in a rough log cabin, where I examined him in his bed. His skin was pale and he was moaning.

Henry lost his sense of time.

In early summer, spring really, there are a few days when the daytime air is warm but the black flies and mosquitoes remain asleep. Lake Huron is still cold; ice floats on the water and snow hides in the tree shadows. Henry had convinced Anselm to swim every one of these days. Unclothed, yelling, running into the water and immediately returning to the beach after the sting of the water. The soft sand absorbed the warmth of the day and radiated it back into the shivering men while they watched the sunset.

September 5, 1849 — I returned to the cabin this morning. Three men lay in their beds, still Henry but now also Fraser Greene and Anselm Laycock. Fraser was in a state of collapse and could hardly speak. Colin and Samuel had died in the night. Their bodies had been moved outside, awaiting burial. On examination, Colin and Samuel's skin shared the grey-blue colour of a death due to cholera.

Henry was sure he saw Anselm climb down from his bunk in the dark at least twice. Was it twice in the same night? Henry tried to ask him if he was feeling well, but his mouth was too dry to speak. He couldn't find the strength to reach down and massage his own knotted calves. He drank the water Anselm brought, or at least tried: he struggled to sit up, and water dribbled across his dry cheeks onto his bed. Henry thought of the time a dog in the village had bitten a porcupine. He and

Anselm had plucked quills out of the poor pup for hours. He thought of the upcoming winter, how cold the cabin would be, how all that is beautiful ends.

Dear colleagues,

I am the medical officer of health for Bruce Mines. Three men in the camp have died of what I believe to be cholera, and the disease is spreading along the north shore of Lake Huron. I am writing to ask if you are knowledgeable of the mode of communication of cholera, or of an effective treatment. I do not believe these deaths to be God's will.

Some of the men share sleeping quarters, but only one in ten have been struck ill. The patients do not cough or itch. Although they work in a copper mine, they are underground for fewer than ten hours each day and generously exposed to fresh air. These are healthy young men who are suddenly struck by loss of fluid from the bowels with no preceding symptoms, followed by fainting, cramping, and oftentimes death.

Your quick reply is sincerely appreciated.

Yours truly,
Wilfred Ulster

The sun shone into the cabin. The hot August weather had abruptly ended while Henry had lain in his bed. The light cut through the cold September wind. For the first time in days — weeks? — Henry did not feel writhing in his bowels. Hunger hit him with a force that made him feel faint. He stood carefully, light-headed. Anselm's bunk was empty. Henry's vision tunnelled, and the cabin threatened to disappear. He was still aware of someone in the cabin. Dr Ulster.

"Where's Anselm?" Henry asked the doctor. The doctor shook his head. "Where's Anselm?" Henry asked again, this time with terror in his voice.

"Gone," the doctor said.

Henry sank back into his bed, wordless.

The doctor lowered his voice. "Gone to God. I understand Anselm ..." He trailed off.

"Anselm knew love," was all Henry could think to say.

THE DRIFT *Part 2*

Jordan Bray

We're delighted to present to you a continuation of Jordan Bray's 'silent' comic, The Drift, the first part of which appeared in Issue 40, Autumn 2023. The full comic, in glorious hardcover, comes out from Wharfinger's Press later this year.

*In his work, **Jordan Bray** attempts to convey the intrigue of the horizon (and grants permission to groan at the pretension). He is drawn to ventures, adventures, and misadventures in strange and interesting places. Jordan has been drawing for the better part of thirty-eight years and is always hunting for that golden balance between passion and profit. Visit him on Instagram @artofjordanbray. Or keep up to date with the book @world_of_the_drift.*

©2025, Jordan Bray

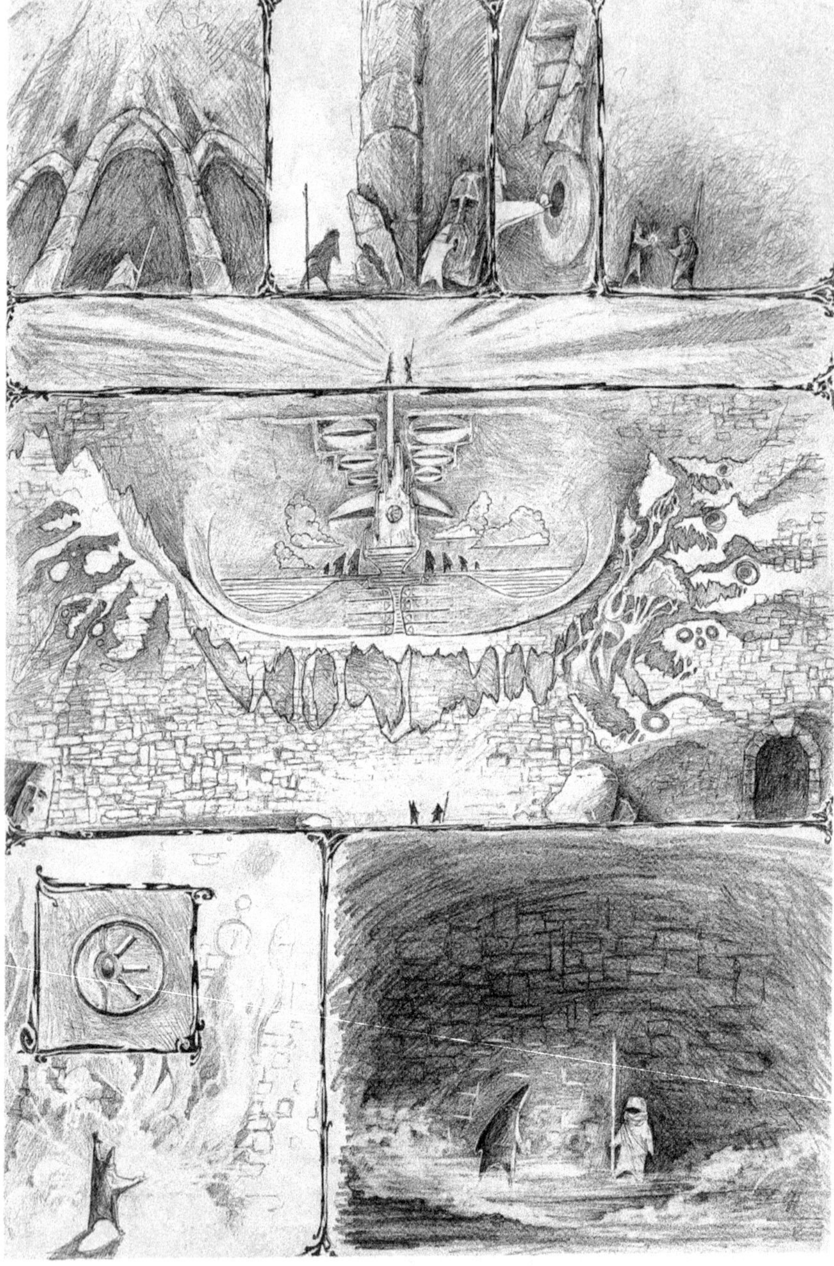

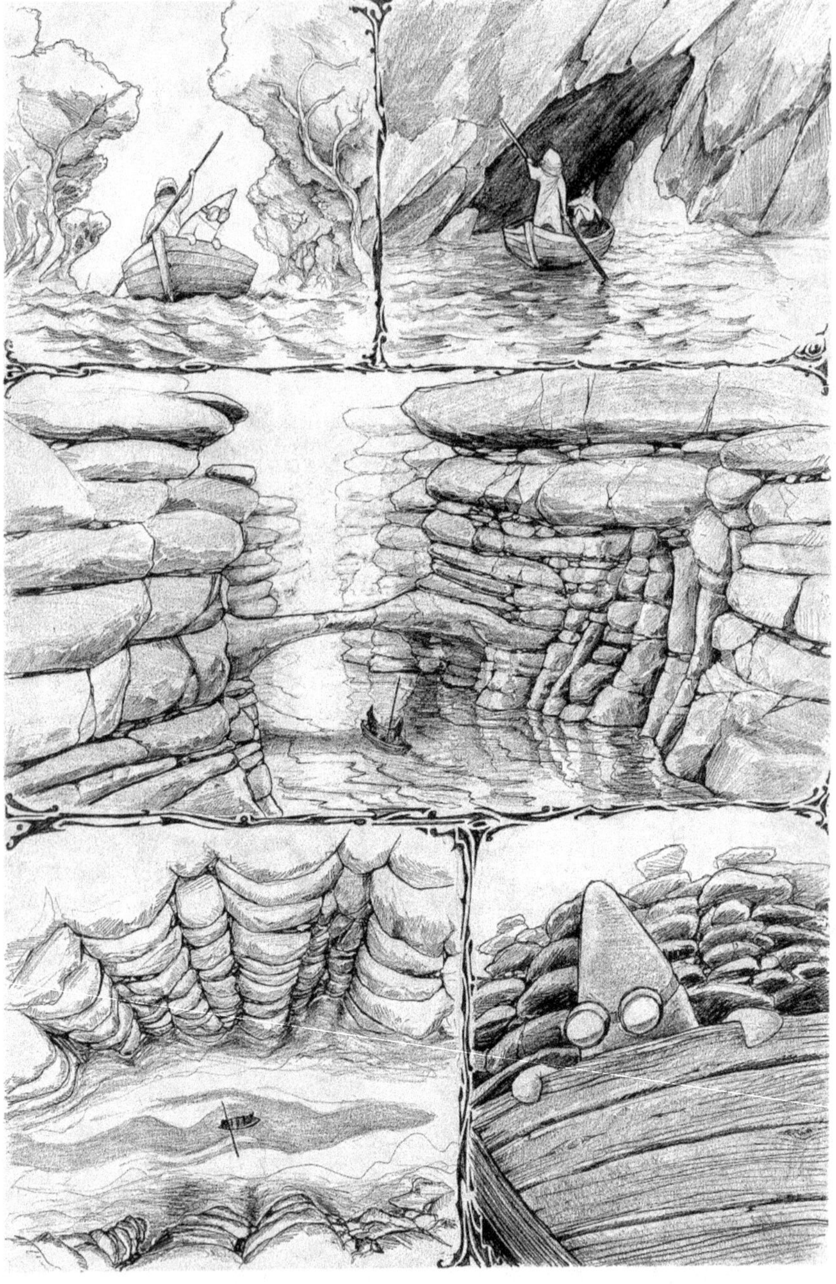

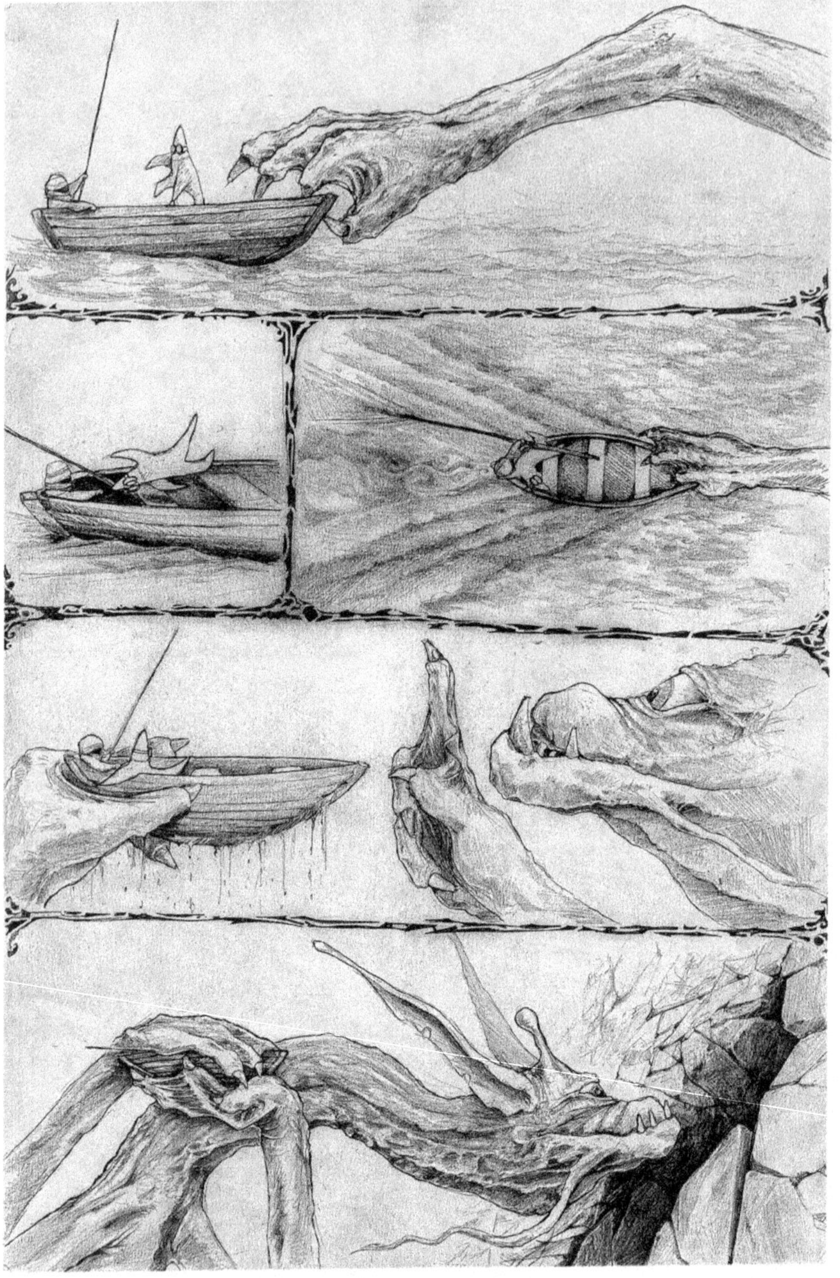

THEIR GRANDFATHER'S CHAIR *Part 2*

JM Landels

JM Landels *is the author of the bestselling Allaigna's Song trilogy as well as the spy novel* The Shepherdess. *'Their Grandfather's Chair', featuring Allaigna's sisters Branwen and Irdina, takes place during the events of* Allaigna's Song: Chorale.

When she's not writing, editing, or drawing, you can find Jen teaching people to swing swords and ride horses at Academie Cavallo in Langley, BC. You can find @jmlandels on most social media platforms, and at jmlandels.stiffbunnies.com.

©2025, JM Landels

Their Grandfather's Chair
Part 2

Previously: Sisters Branwen and Irdina have been sent across the Clearwater Sea on a mission to soften their grandfather's heart and loosen the Mageguard web that entangles his throne. The moment they set foot in Rheran, they become separated when a cadre of Mageguard mistakenly arrests Branwen. Her letter of introduction exonerates her but earns her an unasked-for escort directly to the Bastion without Irdina, who disappeared when the crowd panicked. Meanwhile Irdina is hidden from the Mageguard by Glaignen, the envoy sent to meet the sisters, and the Leisanmira seer Nourd. While Irdina follows Glaignen through the hidden passageways of Rheran to the Bastion, Branwen is already there, awaiting an audience with her grandfather, the Prince High.

It was not Branwen's grandfather who came to the small audience chamber, but his second wife, the Princess High Gwannyn. She was announced by a maid who looked daggers at Branwen as the latter scrambled from her grandfather's chair and gave a quick bow. The Princess made no comment about a stranger in her husband's seat but glided past Branwen's bowing form to sit in the tall-backed chair herself.

Without preamble, she said, "And you are?"

Branwen bowed again and retrieved the letter of introduction from the breast pocket of her jerkin. "Branwen Andreg, Your Highness. His Highness's granddaughter."

The maid took the letter and passed it to her mistress, who didn't comment on the already-broken seal. Gwannyn opened the top fold briefly, then placed the letter on the side table. She stood, her arms open. "I am delighted to meet you at last, my dear." She wrapped her arms around Branwen in a hug perfumed by exotic scents. She stepped back, leaving her hands on Branwen's shoulders. "You have your mother's eyes. But you have a twin sister, do you not? Did she not come with you?"

Branwen looked into the Princess High's large brown eyes and glowing smile, and found the two didn't match. This was not the welcome she had been expecting from her grandfather's wife. For some reason, she felt inclined to lie.

"Irdina had some other business in the city. I came ahead." She gave a quick curtsy, despite her lack of skirts and the Princess's hands still on her shoulders. "It is wonderful to finally meet Your Highness."

"Please, not 'Your Highness'! Call me Grandmama."

The suggestion hit Branwen like a slap to the face. Her father's parents had died long before she was born. Chanist, the Prince High, hadn't visited her home in Teillai since she was three. And she had only just learned, before setting sail for Rheran, that her grandfather's first wife Irdaign, supposedly exiled in Myrwater, was in fact her childhood nurse, Angeley. 'Grandparent' was a complicated term for Branwen and her siblings, but whatever a grandparent might be, it was not this bejewelled princess with the kind smile and cold eyes.

Branwen gave a matching smile and nod that might have been agreement or not, letting the matter slide away without comment. "Is Grandpapa in?"

"He is resting, as he most often does at this hour. But come, you must be exhausted from your journey — sea voyages are so dreadful. Lanyss," she said to her maid, "please have the Fox chamber readied for Branwen and her sister, and bring us a meal in the solar. Come." She took Branwen by the hand, barely giving her time to snatch up her pack, and led her from the audience chamber.

The solar was warm, almost suffocating after the cold wind outside and the unheated halls downstairs. The floor was carpeted from the doorway to the walls in dense gold wool. Large, expensive mirrors reflected the yellow and orange silk that covered the divans, armchairs, and cushions clustered around the room. But despite the rich and sunny furnishings and the heat of the fireplace, the room was chilled by its emptiness.

The solar at Osthegn, though half the size and appointed at a fraction of the cost, was never empty. At any time you might find Branwen's mother, her nurse, one of her many siblings, any number of visiting nobles or servants, and at the very least a gaze hound or two stretched out by the hearth. It was draughty in the winter, when the wind blew from the east and frost glazed the leaded diamonds of the window. But it was warmer than this opulent, overheated, but personless room.

Is she lonely? Branwen thought with sudden sympathy.

Gwannyn invited Branwen to sit at a small table by a window that overlooked the inner courtyard. Branwen propped her pack against the wall and shed her coat without waiting for a servant's help.

Glaignen led Irdina along the winding back streets of Rheran, on what he called a short cut but which already seemed twice as long as the straight High Road. And that was without the sudden stops and about-faces they took each time he spotted a black-cloaked Mageguard.

"They're out in force today," he muttered.

"Why? And why did they take Branwen with them?"

"The latter, I'm not sure. She wasn't a prisoner by the looks of it. But they did have two prisoners with them—"

"Who came off the same ship we did."

"That is the interesting part. Do you think it has anything to do with the death of Osthegn's vizier?"

Irdina cast a sharp look at him, unsure how she should answer. She was under strict instructions not to discuss the events at her home that had killed the castle mage and rendered her mother and eldest sister unconscious—a condition her mother had yet to recover from. How did Glaignen know about it so soon? And how would Rheran's Mageguard have learned of it?

As if he could read her mind, Glaignen put a hand on her shoulder. "Irdaign told me. I'm so very sorry about your mother. How is she?"

Irdina swallowed and nodded. "The same."

He squeezed her shoulder. "At least she is not worse. And your sister Allaigna?"

Irdina shrugged off his hand. "She recovered." Irdina fought back anger at the unfairness—that her sister, whom she barely knew, who had abandoned the family for a half-dozen years, should bring turmoil and death upon her return and yet fare better than their mother.

Glaignen gave an audible sigh. And despite Irdina's obvious desire to avoid his touch, he took her hand. "Don't fret, lass. Your mother is not done with the world yet."

He gave another squeeze and let go, leaving Irdina's gloved hand warm and her half of the puzzle ring tingling. Did she imagine that his voice took on the same tone that Angeley's did when she spoke of the future?

"Your sister Branwen," Glaignen said, moving off again, "has been marked by Kolluk'khan."

"Marked? Who is Kolluk'khan?"

He pulled her into a crooked gap between buildings. She'd lost track of the Bastion, and even their direction of travel, though she suspected from the slope of the ground that they were not climbing the hill but instead moving across it. Had she made the wrong choice in trusting this man, despite her grandmother's name in his mouth? Branwen had headed straight up the hill to the Bastion, and here Irdina was, mucking about in alleyways.

"Kolluk'khan is the vizier, and head of the Mageguard." Glaignen squeezed sideways through an even narrower space, leaving his arm behind to beckon Irdina forward. "It's rare to see her in her blacks on the street rather than in court."

Irdina had to remove her pack to fit through the gap, and claustrophobia gripped her tighter than the walls on either side.

"Did you see how she touched Branwen on the chin?" he asked.

Irdina shook her head, but she was barely paying attention to his words. Instead, she fixed her gaze on the narrow ledge they now stood on, and tried not to fall off. Below them was a fosse, as deep as the house behind her was tall, and a healthy three strides across. On the other side of that, the city wall rose four times higher.

"How are we getting up there?" she asked.

"Not up," he replied. "Down."

Branwen's fingers itched as she patiently held the cup of spiced wine Brandishear's Princess High had just poured with her own hands. Branwen didn't drink at all if she could help it — not wine, not beer, not even cider. Nonetheless, she schooled her face and took polite sips, thinking what a waste of rare oranges it was.

"And how is your dear mother? I'm surprised she didn't write to let us know you were coming."

Branwen took another sip she didn't want while she formulated an answer to skirt subjects she was forbidden to discuss. "Sadly, she has been unwell, but she is recovering. It is one of the reasons we came here — to let Grandpapa know in person. I'm sorry — " She put her cup down slightly too fast. "My stomach doesn't agree with wine so soon after a sea journey, it seems."

It wasn't the wine making her stomach roil, but the increasing unease about Irdina. Yes, she'd left her in the company of Angeley's envoy. But suppose Irdina's temper had caused her to say something untoward — or even attack the man again. Would he still bring her here?

"You poor thing," said Gwannyn. "Your room will be ready soon. I'll have a page draw a bath."

"That's very kind, Your — Grandmama," Branwen said. "But I feel what I need most is a walk in the air. I don't want to take any more of your time. May I walk in the yard until my sister arrives?"

Gwannyn's tone cooled ever so slightly. "The yard is no place for a member of the family, my dear. Take your ease in the cloister gardens. But first, let me show you your room so you can put down your pack."

As Glaignen made his way down the steep walls of the ditch with the ease of a bear cub slipping down a tree, Irdina's anger grew. Her sister had simply walked up to the Bastion, where they both had every right to be, and here she was, being asked to climb into a ditch.

Glaignen called up. "There are handholds. Go straight down, not left or right."

She bellied over the edge and found the first foothold before the smell reached her. She could see streaks along the wall where residents of the tall city houses tossed slops out their windows. Gagging, she hurried down, grateful for her gloves. She dreaded what her feet might find at the bottom, but suddenly her feet found nothing at all.

"It's all right." Glaignen's voice was muffled and distant. "You'll have to drop the last little bit, but I'll catch you."

She looked under her arm to see that he had disappeared from the ledge, and only his hands emerged from what had to be a hole in the stone wall. If he could get down without someone to catch him, so could she.

"Please don't," she said, muscling her way down the last few holds with her hands alone, grateful for the strength in her shoulders from the weapons training she'd been made to do and the stable work she did voluntarily. The final drop was shorter than she anticipated, like vaulting off of a pony when you're used to a hunter, and she jarred her knees and ankles.

Glaignen didn't catch her, but he did extend a hand, which she grasped by the wrist to stop from falling backward. She had to duck to fit into the alcove where he crouched. It was a triangular opening in the stone face, like the head of a boar spear reaching up, where the raw rock of the Bastion's foot met human-made wall. A trickle of water flowed over the side of the ledge she'd landed on, and fell to the ditch below.

She lifted a foot. "Is that … ?"

"Waste water? No," answered Glaignen as she let go of his wrist and adjusted her pack. "It comes from the spring that Brandis captured when he had this fortress built. The old songs say it was part of the bargain he struck with the spirits of the spring — that he had to let part flow unfettered to the Mother Sea, or the water would turn foul." He disappeared further into the crevice. "Come."

Irdina followed, fighting claustrophobia and irritation both.

"I was to bring you both this way to bypass the Mageguard," came Glaignen's voice. "Your ship was hours early."

"We had fairer winds than usual, my sister said. I was too sick to notice."

"No matter. At least we'll get one of you in without Kolluk'khan's mark."

"So this crack in the stone is a route into the keep? And the Mageguard won't notice?" Since the Mageguard had come to her home of Osthegn, the vizier Ashegar had learned of every footprint that came or went from the keep — until she'd died in the arcane fire that had nearly taken Irdina's mother. Irdina forced back the familiar lump in her throat with irate words. "Seems sloppy."

"It's the spring water. According to the legend, none who bear malice to the line of Brandis may pass it."

"That sounds like a fairy tale."

"Perhaps. But perhaps it is fundamental arcana, deeper than our human mages know. What wizard would dare tamper with that?"

"So my grandfather's castle has an unwatched entry, guarded by what … faith?"

"The Bastion has stood for 1 6 0 0 years, and Brandis's heirs have sat on Brandishear's throne the whole time. If the wheel rolls —"

"— don't mend it." Irdina finished the phrase she'd heard hundreds of times from her mother's lips. Which brought another thought to her own. "How many people know of this way in, do you think?"

"Well, I learned of it from your sister Allaigna many years ago. I suspect she learned of it —"

"— from my mother," Irdina interrupted again. She recalled a midwinter fire a year or two before, Branwen lounging beside the hounds on the hearth, their sister Lauriana sorting bright embroidery threads in the basket their mother never had time to use. And their mother, telling stories of her youth in this place: of her cousin Genissa, of her stepmother Gwannyn, of her many suitors before she was sent off to Aerach to marry their father, and of her rebellious year of slipping out of the Bastion to keep low company. Lauriana, impertinent as ever, asked if it was one of that low company that was Allaigna's father.

"Certainly not," was their mother's mild reply. "I kissed many a swain, but I left Brandishear a maiden."

Later, Lauriana said to her sisters, "She never said she arrived in Aerach a maiden."

Irdina was never sure why Lauriana was so determined to prove their oldest sister's illegitimacy when it changed nothing.

But what rested with Irdina now was that her mother, when she left the Bastion to revel in the city, may have followed this very path. Irdina's throat constricted yet again, and yet again, she forced the pain back down with anger.

Alone at last in the room that had been prepared for them, Branwen felt her twin sister's absence even more urgently but was unsure what to do about it. To give herself time to think, she unpacked and aired her sea-damp clothes on the curtained bed. The warmth from the hearth came not from a fire but from a half-dozen evercoals nestled on the grate, and the white winter light from the large-paned windows was supplemented with an evenlamp ensconced beside the door. Arcane heat and light were luxuries they lacked at home in Osthegn, but then it seemed this guest room had richer furnishings than their entire castle.

In addition to the massive bed, there was a pair of well-stuffed armchairs next to a cushioned window seat, a side board stocked with several stoppered decanters, and a polished dark wood table with a gilt bowl full of fresh oranges, figs, and fruit Branwen didn't even recognize. On the opposite wall was a dressing table with an unimaginably expensive looking-glass half as high as she and as wide as her shoulders. There were at least twenty guest rooms in the Bastion — did each of them contain a fragile piece of silvered glass that cost more than a good horse or a half-dozen cattle?

She ran her finger around the polished oak frame, which was composed of stylized foxes that matched the pair engraved on the outside of the room's door. Her mother had told her of the gallery's doors, each one marked by a different animal. They were the work of Seytheral, the architect who had designed the Bastion 1600 years before for Brandis II. But this mirror was newer, for the technique of silvering glass, never mind forming it into large, perfect sheets like this, did not exist in pre-Imperial times.

She put her hand to her chin in thought and felt a tingle in her puzzle ring, like the spark from a cat's fur on a winter day. In response, her chin burned—less like a spark and more like an ember striking the spot the Mageguard had touched. She leaned forward, peering at her chin in the mirror. It looked as it always did except for a blemish on the left side that had been brewing since she boarded the *Lassie*. But the mirrored glass, smooth, flat, and blemishless, *rippled.* Her eyes were not watering; she did not still feel the sway of the ship. The glass surface had undulated like a sheet in a spring breeze.

She touched her index finger to the reflection of her chin and left a greasy smudge on the solid glass. With the sleeve of her left arm, she wiped it clean. Her ring tingled again, her chin burned, and the glass flickered black for the blink of an eye.

She stepped back and saw nothing but her own reflection set in the opulent room. But she felt eyes upon her. A feeling like that of the Mageguard's yellow stare.

An embroidered blanket hung over the foot of the bed. Keeping her eyes on her reflection in the mirror, she reached for the blanket and shook it open. With a duellist's flourish, she fanned it over the looking-glass. It settled over the frame, and the feeling of being watched went out like a snuffed candle.

She breathed, her shoulders relaxing, and turned the ring around on her finger, reverting to her original worry. Where was Irdina? She pulled her boots back on, grabbed her coat, and closed the door of the Fox chamber behind her.

After a solid quarter bell of following Glaignen in darkness that seemed to grow ever more complete, they turned a bend and Irdina could once more see his black silhouette against a bluer darkness. Another turn and there was definitely light ahead: a turquoise glow, greener than the grey winter light they'd left behind.

One more bend, and the passage opened into a cavern lit by glowing blue-green veins in the irregular rock face. And the sound she'd been unable to identify was clear: water rushing from a gap in the cavern's ceiling.

"The Bastion's spring? But it's a fall, not a spring," she said.

"Look again." He pointed at a place where water burbled gently over a lip of rock into the wider pool. "That's the spring. That"—his hand moved towards the fall—"feeds the Bastion."

She peered at the water and it was indeed ... flowing upwards to the crack in the ceiling. "That's some powerful arcana," she said, stepping past him. She pulled off her gloves and put a hand on one of the glowing rock veins. "What is this rock?" Her fingers were a translucent purple, with a hint of bones showing through.

"Iriscite. It's the source that powers magic from beneath the keep."

His voice was just above a whisper. He was no longer the self-assured man who'd led her here, and she noticed he stayed well away from the walls.

"It makes you uncomfortable."

"I'm not family. The fact you don't notice it means you are."

She gave an irritated twitch of her head. She didn't believe in birthright. Inheritance was just a tool used by families like hers to take advantage of everyone else.

He interrupted her musing. "I suggest you strip down to your underthings."

"What!?" Her voice crackled through the quiet.

"I'll hold your pack. The only way past the spring is through, and you'll need to get wet head to toe."

Branwen tried not to be distracted by the opulent beauty of the gallery level on which her room sat. She kept her gaze forward and only slightly down, her step purposeful but not hurried—looking, she hoped, like neither a tourist nor a spy. Gwannyn had led her here from the solar to the north, but the kitchen was Branwen's goal now.

The south end of the gallery had stairs leading down to a gently curving corridor with large glazed windows on one side and shuttered arrow slits on the other. She passed several servants and courtiers along the way, maintaining the unapproachable mien that kept her unnoticed. She wished she had a tray to carry to make her seem like she belonged, but even after changing from her travelling clothes, she looked nothing like the neatly tabarded pages and staff she'd seen. As she crossed by the main entrance, she spotted the porter who had admitted her and her Mageguard escort. And, unfortunately, he saw her too.

He gave a short bow. "Are you lost, mistress?" he asked.

She'd never been addressed as 'mistress' in her life. With her anonymity gone, she'd have to make the most of it. She lifted her chin and gave him what she hoped was an imperious gaze, speaking with more command than she felt. "The kitchen garden, good man. Where is it?" It was hard not to feel as if the Mageguard's thumbprint glowed on her chin.

He took her by the elbow — politely, of course — and turned her towards the door opposite the entrance. "Surely you'd rather the glass garden, milady," he said. "It's the only one worth looking at this time of year."

She allowed him to usher her into a cloistered walk. He gestured across manicured parterres to a glass-walled structure on the north wall of the courtyard.

"Please enjoy the heated gardens. But keep the doors closed so the birds don't escape."

She thanked him and made her dutiful way towards the glasshouse, no longer amazed by the sheer amount of glazing in the castle. On her way, she cast an eye towards the brick wall that separated her from a group of chimneys wafting smoke and the scents of roast meat and baking bread. The kitchen garden was certainly on the other side of that wall. But with no entry to it, her only choice was the glasshouse. She turned the wrought-iron handle of its door, and was assaulted by a wall of steam that rolled over her.

The chatter of birdsong was shocking in the midst of winter, as was the collage of gigantic many-coloured blossoms, all unfamiliar to her. Bright creatures never seen in Aerach flitted from broad-leafed plants and blooming vines, and the warm, moist air caressed her salt-stung lips and cheeks. As stunning and luxurious as it was, however, her need for escape was stronger. There was a small wooden door in the brick wall to her left, but it lacked a handle.

Back out into the winter cold she went, and strode to the cloister walk. Without glancing at the porter, she turned right. Enough skulking. She was granddaughter to the Prince.

She marched into the kitchens, which were easy to find from the noise and aroma, crossed the busy staging area without heed to the cooks, servers, and pages who crowded it, and opened the door to the garden.

"Close that door!" yelled a cook. "The pudding will sink!"

She obliged, stepping into the cool of a winter garden. There, where Angeley had said it would be, was the fountain. Not a fancy one like that in the courtyard: just a pipe, with water gurgling into a deep basin. Water from the basin overflowed into a metal grate at its base.

Below that, she reckoned, must be the outflow. "If you need to leave without being noticed," Angeley had told them, "follow the spring's path from the kitchen garden."

She eyed the grate sceptically. Was it new? For she'd have to be water herself to fit through the grille. She glanced over her shoulder at the kitchens. The door remained closed, and the windows were too high for casual gazing.

A fringe of clinging grass held the grille fast at her first attempt to lift it. She dug her knife tip around the edge, scraped away the grass in a strip she'd be able to put back, and the grate came away, sending a shower of surrounding pea gravel plinking into water below. There were iron rungs set into the brick wall, which extended well below ground level. It seemed a long way down for a catch basin. The steady trickle of water from the fountain flowed down one side of the rectangular hole, and the rungs were on the other.

She cast another look around to see if she was being watched, but the wall's abutment hid her partly from the kitchen, and the overhang that sheltered the fountain obscured most of the view from the castle windows. Seeing no reasonable excuse to delay further, she peered into the dark chimney and swung a leg down, feeling for the first rung.

And then she heard something—a voice she recognized better than her own. She couldn't hear words, but the tone was familiar: curt, irritated, impolitic. The voice moved closer and clearer, till she could see Irdina's green hat far below and hear her utter more courteous thanks.

"The water needs to touch all of you," Glaignen said.

"Then shouldn't I take off my underclothes as well?" she challenged.

"Only if they're waterproof. You can leave more on if you like. It depends how wet you want to be on the other side."

She made him turn his back while she stripped down to her chemise and linen braies in the cold, damp air. In the end she decided to take the braies off too. Her chemise reached to mid-thigh, and there was no sense getting more clothes wet than necessary. She stuffed her dryish clothes into her pack and stuck her green felt hat to the top with one of her hat pins.

"This water that will raise an alarm if I'm not soaked in it—won't it object to my dry pack?"

"Not if you're carrying it. Which is why I'm going to hand it to you after your dip."

She nodded. It made a certain amount of sense, as much as magic ever did. Shivering in the clammy air, she braced herself for the shock of colder water on her cold feet. But it was warm—not like bathwater, but the same temperature as her body. She waded in deeper. It felt, in fact, like nothing at all, or at most like a warm summer breeze swirling round her ankles. It barely resisted her as she waded out, and she couldn't wait to reach deeper water.

She ducked her head under and had to remind herself not to breathe the water that felt so much like air. Her half of the puzzle ring glowed on her finger like the rock veins. She slid it forward to her knuckle, remembering Angeley's admonishment never to remove it without Branwen's half, and then tucked it back into place once the water had soaked the skin beneath.

It was with reluctance that she stood, the cold air assaulting her wet skin. She kept her back to Glaignen, conscious that her shift was now translucent and clinging to her admittedly unvoluptuous frame.

"Coat," she said, holding out her hand behind her when she had backed up to the edge of the spring. Once she had her calf-length coat on over her dripping shift, she felt less vulnerable.

"That ring," Glaignen said, catching her left hand. "It's Lei-sanmira. Who has the other half?"

"Branwen," she said.

He nodded. "Just as well you came into the palace separately. Don't get those two halves close together in the presence of the Mageguard if you can help it."

She felt her anger grow again: at her grandfather, for allowing Mageguard into his seat, for being no better than the power-jealous dukes and princes of Aerach; at Angeley, for sending her on this precarious quest with less knowledge than this stranger — or anyone else, for that matter — seemed to have, as if a pair of adolescent girls could throw a bar into the carriage wheels of power; and, irrationally, at Branwen, for taking the easy route into the Bastion under Mageguard escort.

Glaignen gave her a detailed description of the path out to the kitchen gardens, though he confessed he knew it only as told to him by others.

Her fury built as she pinned her hat back onto her sopping hair. She shouldered her pack, its weight pressing new coldness from the wet fabric of her shift onto her back.

"So this is the 'escort' I get?" Her voice started to rise. "A trip through the bowels of the city, and now it's left, right, climb a ladder, and hope not to get arrested when I stick my head above ground?" She snatched up her boots and strode back into the spring, tucking her coattails under her arm. She splashed around the perimeter, where the water was shallow, and landed up on the far side. She hopped on one foot, dragging a boot on over wet skin.

He called across the water, his voice soft but clear. "Do you doubt your abilities?"

She glared at him in the dim turquoise light as she struggled with the second boot. *Yes,* she wanted to shout. She wanted to scream in anger and cry in fear.

"Fuck no," she yelled back. "I just doubt everyone else."

He laughed, his teeth glinting green. "Good!"

She spun on her heel and had to reach a hand to the blue-veined rock to steady herself on the shale path.

"And good luck," he called after her.

"I don't need your damned luck!" She let out a string of curses, many of them learned shipboard, as she scrambled up the rocky path, shivering violently. She reached the first rough-hewn stair, paused, and called back in a more polite voice, "But thank you."

§

To be continued in Pulp Literature *Issue 47, Summer 2025.*

For more high fantasy, family drama, and political intrigue set in the lands of the Ilmar, check out the spellbinding Allaigna's Song trilogy from JM Landels at Pulp Literature Press. https://pulpliterature.com/allaignas-song/

NOW AVAILABLE!

THE MAGICAL CONCLUSION TO THE MUST-READ EPIC TRILOGY

the adventures of Allaigna sing

simply a joy to read

keeps you turning pages from beginning to end

an immensely satisfying epic

PULPLITERATURE.COM/ALLAIGNAS-SONG/

THE ARTISTS

Steve R Gagnon
Cover artist, Towton

A graphic designer by trade, Steve R Gagnon majored in illustration and graduated from the Université de Laval in Québec in 1987. An acclaimed creative and art director in the advertising world, he is drawn more and more to his first loves: painting, drawing, and sculpture. He has a particular interest in history and images that transport the viewer to another time and place. Our cover image, *Towton,* showing a raven perched on a mediaeval longsword, is from the series Battles and Aftermaths, which juxtaposes the implacable finality of war against the delicate resilience of nature. His painting *Vimy,* from the same series, was the cover of *Pulp Literature* Issue 24, Autumn 2019. Find more of Steve's work on Instagram @stevergagnon.

Jordan Bray
Illustrator, The Drift

Jordan Bray has always sought a place in the career world, where he can immerse himself in creativity. Alas, this world often thrives on chaos and uncertainty, so he busies himself making strange and unique things for the film industry and for clients who figure, 'Guess it doesn't hurt to ask.'

While travelling in Sydney, Australia, Jordan had a sudden anomalous desire for some visual world building. In his frenzy, he bought a stack of huge paper and a drawing board and, on a threadbare couch in a hostel, drew the first four pages. With no real direction in mind save for a brave protagonist setting off to discover what lies beyond the edge of what he knows, Jordan set out to explore 'what lies beyond the drift'.

As his debut graphic adventure grew from a place of escapist wonder to an epic tale, Jordan began to feel the love that comes from the intimate familiarity of a story and its world. He fell in love with the process of learning new ways to tell that story. This is the second instalment of *The Drift*, which first appeared in Issue 40 of *Pulp Literature*. The full 105-page tale is finally being released by Wharfinger's Press mid-2025.

Mel Anastasiou
In-house illustrator
Mel Anastasiou loves drawing for *Pulp Literature* because she loves the stories she illustrates. She draws in black and white, working from imagination and inspired by details from Renaissance compositions. You can find illustrations, writing tips, and news about her books and novellas at melanastasiou.wordpress.com, and see more of her artwork on Facebook at Bird and Branch Artwork.

HALL OF FAME

These are the heroes——the Patrons and Pulp Literati whose monthly support helped bring you this issue. Please lift your glasses and give them a rousing cheer!

The Brewers
Dana Tye Rally

The Innkeepers
Abigail Bruce
Andrea Kepple
David Jensen
Ev Bishop
Gilles Cyrenne
Gillian Gardiner
Kevin Harris
Lorna Ens
Mark Francis
Richard Ohnemus
Robin McGillveray
Susan Jackson
Kevin S Moul

The Cicerones
Bjarne Hansen
Jennifer Sommersby
Roger & Anne Anastasiou
Zoë Ricard

The Bartenders
Alana Krider
Andrea Kirkham
Anna Belkine
Brighton Hugg
Bryan Moose
Chris Olee
Dave Wayne
Deepthi Atukorala
Dena Linn Chen
Devan Erno
Ernst Pulido
Evelyn Ann
Finnian Burnett
Hannah Moor
James Carlino
Jennifer Getsinger
Jillian Shoichet
Kat Hankinson
Katherine Derbyshire
kc dyer
Kelsey Brennan
Kenneth W Gardner

Kim Seary
KT Wagner
Leny Wagner
Lin & John Richardson
Margot Landels
Margot Spronk
Megan Shaw
Michelle Balfour
Mike Sylvester
Peter Halasz
Rapscallion
Regina Rogers
Richard Gropp
Ron Graves
Scott F Gray
Shannon Saunders
Star
Suzanne Philip
Venasa Simpson

The Regulars

Adam Fout
Alice Rhoades
Andy W
BC
Brandi Estey-Burtt
Catherine Levinson
Charity Tahmaseb
Emmy Bee
James Gotaas
Jenny Blackford
JS Andrew
Marilyn Holt
Marilyn K
Marta Salek
Meredith Frazier
Michelle Robinson
Paul Anguiano
Rina Piccolo
Sonia Brock
Vera

If you would like to join the ranks of these worthies, you can become a patron on Patreon at patreon.com/pulplit or join the Pulp Literati through our website at pulpliterature.com/join-pulp-literati/

MCNALLY ROBINSON BOOKSELLERS & PRAIRIE FIRE WRITING CONTESTS

2025 ANNUAL WRITING CONTESTS

$3,750
IN CASH PRIZES!

ONE CASH PRIZE OF $1,250 IN EACH CATEGORY

MRB POETRY CONTEST

(up to 3 poems per entry, max. 150 lines total)

Judge: Tolu Oloruntoba

MRB SHORT FICTION CONTEST

(one story per entry, max. 5,000 words)

Judge: Shashi Bhat

MRB CREATIVE NON-FICTION CONTEST

(one piece per entry, max. 5,000 words)

Judge: Basma Kavanagh

DEADLINE:
NOV. 30, 2025

FEE: $34 per entry, which includes a one-year subscription to *Prairie Fire.*

Image by Freepik

prairiefire

McNALLY ROBINSON

Complete guidelines at
www.prairiefire.ca
For inquiries: prfire@prairiefire.ca

The Malahat Review

ESSENTIAL POETRY • FICTION • CREATIVE NONFICTION

Constance Rooke
Creative Nonfiction Prize

PRIZE MONEY
$1250

ENTRY DEADLINE
August 1, 2025

ENTRY FEE
$35

Commit these deadlines to memory

November 1, 2025
Open Season Awards │ $6000
Three writers split the winnings

February 1, 2026
Novella Prize │ $2000
One winner earns the prize

May 1, 2026
Far Horizons Award
for Poetry │ $1250
One winner takes the prize

University
of Victoria

malahatreview.ca
malahat@uvic.ca

OPENS: MAR. 1
DEADLINE: JUN. 2

The winning submission will
also be published in issue 305
of *The Fiddlehead*, Autumn 2025!

$2000 Prize!

MEET OUR JUDGE:

Nicole Breit is a queer, award-winning essayist and creative development coach based on the traditional lands of the Sḵwx̱wú7mesh people in Gibsons, BC. Her writing has been widely published in journals and anthologies. When she isn't writing, Nicole mentors emerging and seasoned creative nonfiction authors through her Spark Your Story programs. **Find her at nicolebreit.com**

NICOLE BREIT

For more information:
thefiddlehead.ca | thefiddlehead.ca/contest | fiddlehd@unb.ca

ARC POETRY

Canada's poetry magazine for over 45 years

3 issues per year, in Spring, Summer, and Fall
$40 for one year
$65 for two years*
subscribe online at
arcpoetry.ca

*Subscription rates listed for Canadian subscribers

 @ Arc Poetry Magazine  @ arcpoetrymag

subTerrain
MAGAZINE

THE 23RD ANNUAL

LUSH

TRIUMPHANT LITERARY AWARDS

Fiction * Poetry
Creative Non-Fiction

$3000
IN CASH PRIZES

DEADLINE FOR ENTRIES: MAY 15, 2025

"It could best be described as 'unafraid'
and as a result has some interesting surprises."
— THE BLOG CANADIAN MAGAZINES

INFORMATION: subterrain.ca

ENTRY FEE: $30
(includes a one-year subscription to subTerrain Magazine)
No simultaneous submissions

Do you have a **story to tell?**
We can help!

Dreamers is dedicated to heartfelt writing. Visit our site for:

- Therapeutic Writing
- Poems & Stories
- Content Marketing
- Creative Nonfiction
- Writing Workshops
- Contests & Anthologies
- Residencies & Retreats
- ...and so much more!

www.DreamersWriting.com

Get on board with *Bookworm* for your *free* weekly dose of exclusive reviews, book excerpts, and much more.

Visit *reviewcanada.ca/TTC* or scan the code to the right.

Literary Review of Canada

A JOURNAL OF IDEAS

IGNITE YOUR
IMAGINATION

30 yrs of award-winning sci-fi and fantasy

WWW.ONSPEC.CA

Keep it weird. Subscribe today!

MARKETPLACE

Books

Advent *by Michael Kamakana* • We thought we knew what the aliens wanted. Think again. pulpliterature.com/advent

Allaigna's Song: Chorale *by JM Landels* The long-awaited conclusion to the bestselling *Allaigna's Song* trilogy. pulpliterature.com/allaignas-song

The Extra: A Monument Studios Mystery *by Mel Anastasiou* • Extra Frankie Ray gets her big break on the Silver Screen, until murder steals the scene. pulpliterature.com/the-extra

The Labours of Mrs Stella Ryman: Further Fairmount Mysteries *by Mel Anastasiou* • Trapped in a down-at-the-heels care home. You'd be cranky too. pulpliterature.com/stella-ryman-and-the-fairmount-manor-mysteries

What the Wind Brings *by Matthew Hughes* • Winner of the 2020 Endeavour Award • pulpliterature.com/product-category/novels/matthew-hughes

The Writer's Boon Companion *by Mel Anastasiou* • Thirty Days Towards an Extraordinary Volume • pulpliterature.com/subscribe/the-bookstore

Bookstores

Russell Books • 100-747 Fort St, Victoria, BC • russellbooks.com

Western Sky Books • 2132-2850 Shaughnessy St, Port Coquitlam, BC V3C 6K5 • 604-461-5602 store.westernskybooks.com

White Dwarf / Dead Write Books 3715 10th Ave W, Vancouver, BC V6R 2G5 • 604-228-8223 whitedwarf@deadwrite.com

Conferences & Events

Surrey International Writers' Conference • 24–26 October 2025 • siwc.ca

When Words Collide • August 2025 Calgary, AB • whenwordscollide.org

Wine Country Writers' Festival • Sep 2025 • winecountrywritersfestival.ca

Writing Resources

Dreamers Creative Writing Workshops • residencies • contests & more • www.dreamerswriting.com

Federation of BC Writers Workshops • contests • networking & more • www.bcwriters.ca/join-us

Amazing Stories • Back in print!
amazingstories.com

Arc Poetry Magazine • Poetry, essays,
interviews, reviews • arcpoetry.ca

EVENT Magazine • Poetry & prose
eventmagazine.ca

Fiddlehead & SCL • Poetry, fiction,
non-fiction
https://thefiddlehead.ca/

Geist • Ideas + Culture • Made in
Canada • geist.com

Literary Review of Canada • Reviews
on everything from policy and politics
to history, biography, and fiction
https://reviewcanada.ca

Malahat Review • Poetry, fiction,
creative non-fiction
www.malahatreview.ca

OnSpec • The Canadian magazine of
the fantastic
onspecmag.wordpress.com

Polar Borealis • Paying market for
new Canadian SF&F writers & artists
polarborealis.ca

Prairie Fire • A Canadian magazine
of new writing • prairiefire.ca

Room Magazine • Literature, Art &
Feminism since 1975
roommagazine.com

Spadina Literary Review • An international quarterly based in Toronto
spadinaliteraryreview.com

SubTerrain Magazine • Fiction,
poetry, photography, and graphic
illustration from uprising Canadian,
US, and International writers and
artists • https://www.subterrain.ca/

Printing & Publishing

Fraser Printers • Surrey's Quality
Printer • fraserprinters.bc.ca

CONTESTS

Pulp Literature runs six annual contests for poetry, flash fiction, short stories, and novel first pages. For contest guidelines, prizes, and entry fees, see pulpliterature.com/contests.

The Hummingbird Flash Fiction Prize
Contest opens: 1 May 2025
Deadline: 15 June 2025
Winner notified: 15 July 2025
Winner published: Issue 49, Winter 2026
Prize: $300

The First Page Cage
Contest opens: 1 August 2025
Deadline: 15 September 2025
Winner notified: 15 October 2025
Quarter-finalists published online: Autumn 2025
Prize: $300

The Raven Short Story Contest
Contest opens: 1 September 2025
Deadline: 15 October 2025
Winner notified: 15 November 2025
Winner published: Issue 50, Spring 2026
Prize: $300

The Kingfisher Poetry Prize
Contest opens: 1 October 2025
Deadline: 15 November 2025
Winner notified: 15 December 2025
Winner published: Issue 50, Spring 2026
Prize: $300

The Bumblebee Flash Fiction Contest
Contest opens: 1 January 2026
Deadline: 15 February 2026
Winner notified: 15 March 2026
Winner published: Issue 51, Summer 2026
Prize: $300

The Magpie Award for Poetry
Contest opens: 1 March 2026
Deadline: 15 April 2026
Winner notified: 15 May 2026
Winner published: Issue 52, Autumn 2026
Prize: $500

"IF A STORY IS IN YOU, IT HAS TO COME OUT."
–William Faulkner

Does your soul yearn to be heard? Let it find its audience at the Spadina Literary Review. Our publication is now open to submissions from heartfelt and earnest writers and artists. Whether you are a student of life, a victim of it, or merely an observant bystander, we invite you to submit to our humble literary magazine.

From an essay about your favourite tree to a memoir about your best friend's last days with cancer, the Spadina Literary Review accepts all your art has to offer. We remain free to read and free to submit to, for our goal is to nurture the diversity of good writing in Canada and to support writers wherever they are.

SO DIG THROUGH YOUR NOTEBOOKS AND BE A PART OF THIS EXTRAORDINARY LITERARY JOURNEY!

To find our submission guidelines and read some great writing, visit SpadinaLiteraryReview.com or simply SpadLit.com

Six awards for genre-busting
fiction and poetry

The Bumblebee Flash Fiction Contest

Deadline: 15 February
Prize: $300

The Magpie Award for Poetry

Deadline: 15 April
First Prize: $500

The Hummingbird Flash Fiction Prize

Deadline: 15 June
Prize: $300

The First Page Cage

Deadline: 30 September
Prize: $300

The Raven Short Story Contest

Deadline: 15 October
Prize: $300

The Kingfisher Poetry Prize

Deadline: 15 October
Prize: $300

become our
2,000TH MEMBER!

The Federation of BC Writers is on the brink of reaching an incredible milestone. Soon, we'll be 2,000 members strong!

To celebrate, we're gifting the 2,000th member of our literary community a free pass to an upcoming Writing Intensive of their choice.

Plus, the member who refers the 2,000th registrant will also enjoy a free spot in a Writing Intensive.

Join us and reap the myriad benefits of a FBCW membership. For a complete list, visit:
bcwriters.ca/benefits

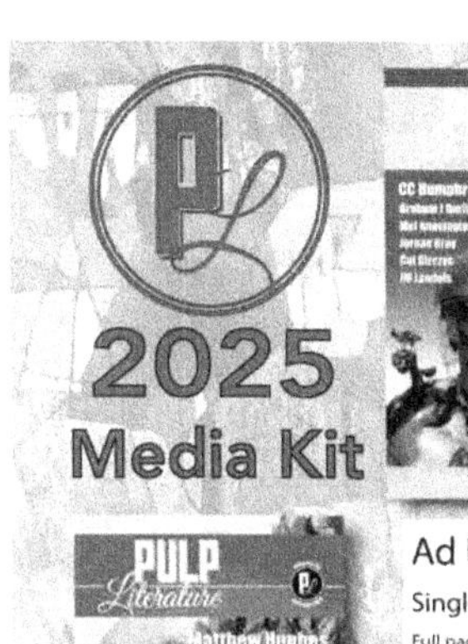

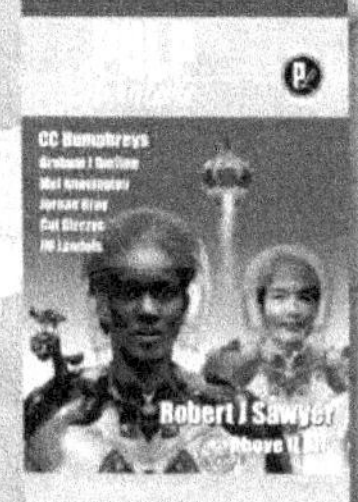

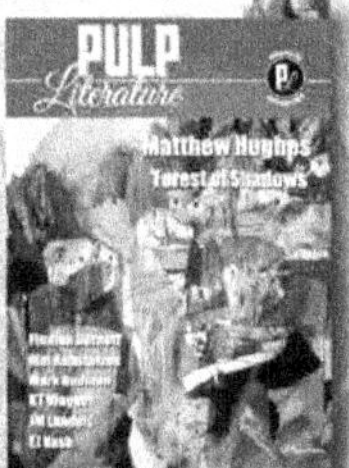

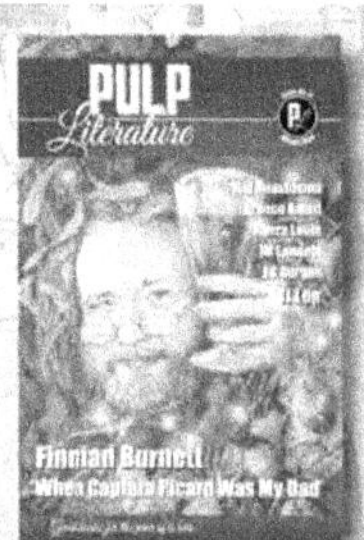

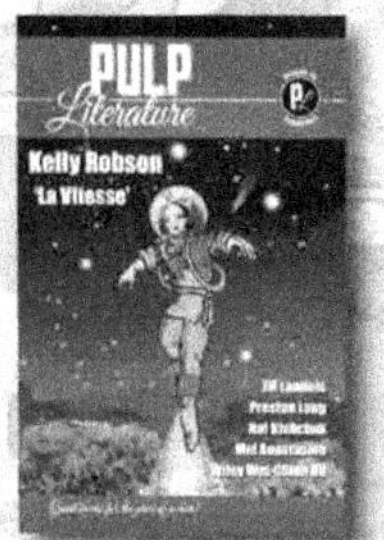

2025
Media Kit
PULP Literature
CC Humphreys
Robert J Sawyer
Finnian Burnett
When Captain Picard Was My Dad
Kelly Robson
'La Vitesse'
Matthew Hughes
Forest of Shadows
Ad Rates
Single Issue
Full page: $250
Half page: $200
Quarter page: $100
Directory (3 text lines): $25
Four Issues
Full page: $795
Half page: $495
Quarter page: $375
Directory (3 text lines): $80
Ad Rates Weekly Digital Newsletter
Our digital weekly newsletter reaches an engaged audience of 2,000 subscribers. With a 54% open rate, our readers consistently interact with and trust the stories, tips, and insights we share.
One Newsletter: $40 | Two Newsletters: $70 | Three Newsletters: $90
Advertise With Us
Full and half-page ads in our quarterly print come with a free directory listing to maximizie your visibility.
To book your ad or learn more, send us an email: info@pulpliterature.com or visit our website at: https://pulpliterature.com/advertise/

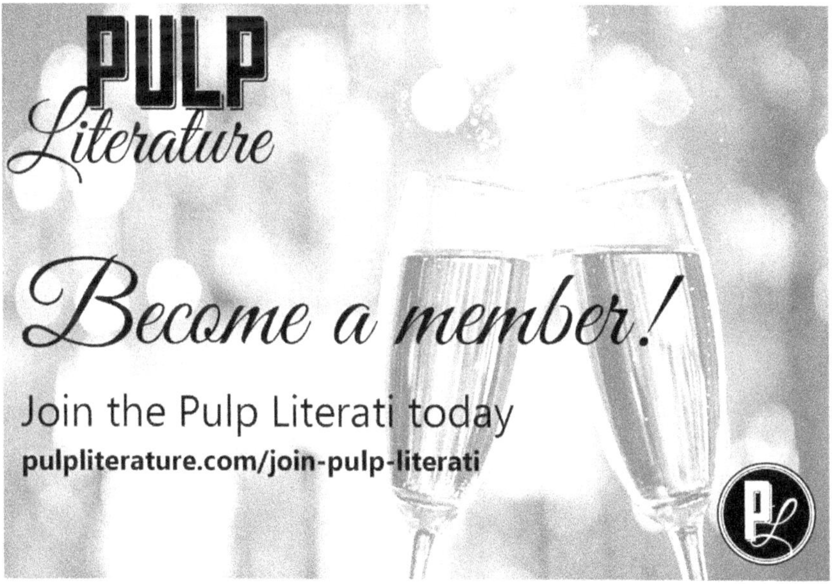
PULP
Literature
Become a member!
Join the Pulp Literati today
pulpliterature.com/join-pulp-literati

"The conjugal blend of mystery and Hollywood atmosphere works on every level. Very highly recommended."

PULPLITERATURE.COM/THE-EXTRA-A-MONUMENT-STUDIOS-MYSTERY

Out of the fires of a Caribbean slave revolt, shipwrecked on the jungle coast of 16th-century Ecuador, an educated slave, a shaman, and a monk hunted by the Inquisition fight for freedom against the might of Imperial Spain.

Dive into an epic slipstream novel of intrigue and adventure from fantasy author Matthew Hughes, the writer George R.R. Martin calls 'criminally underrated,' and Robert J. Sawyer says is 'a towering talent.'

'A triumph!' - Cecelia Holland
'Sensational' - Candas Jane Dorsey

pulpliterature.com

Fantastic Fresh Fiction!

PULP
Literature

Become a Patron of *Pulp Literature*

By supporting *Pulp Literature* on Patreon with $2 or more per month, you will be laying the foundation for a secure future for the magazine, as well as ensuring that you never miss an issue! Your subscription includes four big issues of short stories, novellas, poetry, comics, and novel excerpts, delivered to your door or electronic mailbox each year. **Find us at patreon.com/pulplit**

If you prefer to subscribe through our website, go to pulpliterature.com/subscribe.

Or you can send a cheque with the form below to
Subscriptions, Pulp Literature Press, 21955 16 Ave, Langley BC, V2Z 1K5, Canada

Don't miss an issue!

❑   **Send me 2 years (8 issues) at the special rate of $110** (save $34)*
❑   **Send me 1 year (4 issues) for $60** (save $12)*
❑   **Send me 2 years of digital issues for $35** (save $12.92)
❑   **Send me 1 year of digital issues for $20** (save $3.96)

Name: ____

Address: ____

City: _________________________________ Prov. / State: _________

Postal code: ______________ Country:_______________________

Email: ____

❑   **Payment enclosed**
❑   **Bill me**
❑   **New**
❑   **Renewal**

Make cheques payable in Canadian funds to Pulp Literature Press. Include email address for digital editions and Paypal billing, or subscribe at www.pulpliterature.com/subscribe.

*for postage outside Canada add $20 per year in North America or $32 per year overseas.

www.ingramcontent.com/pod-product-compliance
Lightning Source LLC
Chambersburg PA
CBHW060408310726
48976CB00003B/979